I0760899

SPILLING INNOCENT BLOOD

Commonwealth Books Classics by James Haddad

Eyes of a Child
The Moledet Solution
The Cracking Foundation
Send Him An Angel
Pier Shock
Boy
56th Street
Cracka Willie
Spilling Innocent Blood

Nonfiction Books

The Middle East Lebanese Diet & Lifestyle

SPILLING INNOCENT BLOOD

Fake Friends, True Friends, or Cowards

JAMES W. HADDAD

Commonwealth Books Inc.,

A Commonwealth Publications Hardback
SPILLING INNOCENT BLOOD
This edition published 2024 by
Commonwealth Books

Published in the United States by Commonwealth Books Inc., New York.

Library of Congress Cataloging-in-Publication Data

Names: Haddad, James, author.
Title: Spilling innocent blood: fake friends, true friends, or cowards / James W. Haddad.
Description: First Commonwealth Books hardback edition. | New York: Commonwealth Books, Inc., 2024.
Identifiers: LCCN 2024024126 (print) | LCCN 2024024127 (ebook) |
ISBN 9781892986542 (hardback) | ISBN 9781892986559 (epub)
Subjects: LCGFT: Thrillers (Fiction) | Detective and mystery fiction. |
Novels. Classification: LCC PS3558.A31175 S65 2024 (print) | LCC
PS3558.A31175
(ebook) | DDC 813/.54--dc23/eng/20240603
LC record available at https://lccn.loc.gov/2024024126LC ebook record
available at https://lccn.loc.gov/2024024127

ISBN: 978-1-892-98654-2 (HARDBACK)
ISBN: 978-1892-986559 (EPUB)

This work is a novel but there are similarities to actual persons or events and based on facts.

First Commonwealth Books Hardback Edition January, 2024

PUBLISHED BY COMMONWEALTH BOOKS, INC.,
www.commnwealthbooks@aol.com
www.commonwealthbooksinc.com
Manufactured in the United States of America

This book is dedicated to the memory of Cody Clayville who died the most unjust death imaginable.

At the hands of cowarads

and

whose friends were enemies

Black on black murder has been occurring since the beginning of time. Today the Blacks are spreading their murderous tentacles outside of their ghetto and spilling white blood. The killing of a white man by a black man is looked upon by the black community as a status symbol. The more a black man kills Whites, the more status he gets. He is looked upon as a hero, a savior of the black people

A bullet in da head make you dead
And if ya white it be right

An African-American ghetto phrase for killing Whites

The ghetto Blacks have exemplified their hatred toward Whites, through their rappers, racists and black supremacists

CODY CLAYVILLE'S DEATH WAS a knife in the heart to his mother. It was a nightmare from which she would never awaken. At about three in the morning, she got a call from Jackson Memorial Hospital telling her, that her son had an accident and to come to the hospital. That was all they told her. She had no reason to even remotely think her son was dead, murdered, abandoned by his friends, left to die on the floor of an interracial party, attended by the trash of society. What other horror could have befallen this young man, as innocent as a stranger walking along a street?

Sleepily, nervously, she got into the car and her boyfriend started driving her to the hospital, along with Cody's girlfriend. Had she known her only son was dead, like any decent parent, she probably would have committed suicide on the spot.

Not much was said as the car headed to the hospital.

It was a long and nerve-wracking ride from the tiny city of Okeechobee to the cesspool City of Miami, where every scumbag in the world congregated, a good hundred miles. With each passing mile, Cody's mother started falling victim to nervous tension. It seemed to be slowly breaking her down, but she constantly fought it off.

She could not let her son see her in a nervous wreck.

The last time Cody was in the hospital was for a heart infection caused from too much of a contaminated drug. But since then, Cody had straightened out his life: he had an apartment, had a girlfriend, had a job, and most importantly, stopped selling drugs and robbing other plugs, drug dealers, at gunpoint. She breathed a sigh of relief. Her only son, and only child on her side of the Clayville family, was finally becoming a man.

He still had a few improvements to make like everyone else in this world. The first and foremost improvement was extremely crucial: stop hanging with people of lesser intelligence or to put it bluntly, *the scum of the earth.*

After the two hour drive the car pulled into the parking lot of the massive hospital. They walked straight to the emergency room. They checked in, explained who they were, who they came to see. They were told to have a seat and the doctor would be with them shortly.

Cody's mother was on edge. She felt grimness in the voice and in the air. She looked nervously at her boyfriend then at Cody's girlfriend.

"Relax. Take it easy," her boyfriend said.

"He's right," Cody's girlfriend said. "Everything will be okay."

Heels were clacking down the hallway, and they stared. It was the doctor. He held a grim look on his face, was avoiding eye contact with everybody. He straightened his glasses, kept a downward gaze. He hated this part of his job. Sometimes he hated even being a doctor. There was no other alternative. He had to break the disturbing news.

They had not even taken a seat before the doctor was standing before them.

The doctor readjusted his glasses. It seemed like he was stalling before breaking the news.

At this point Cody's mother sensed a tragedy. She could feel it and a strange fear was sweeping through her limbs. She was doing everything she could not to collapse.

The doctor wasted no more time. He was staring directly at Cody's mother.

"We did everything we could to save his life," the doctor said. "He was airlifted to the hospital. That's how bad of shape he was in."

"You mean he is no longer with us?" Cody's mother uttered in disbelief.

The doctor tried to look sad as he shook his head positively.

Cody's mother, girlfriend and stepfather were numb with grief and shock. They could not believe it. They were told Cody had an accident and to come to the hospital and here they were, and Cody was dead.

"What happened?" Cody's mother practically screamed. "What happened to my son?"

"He was shot four times either in the chest and the bullets exited the back or in the back and the bullets exited his chest," the doctor explained in great detail. "He died about three hours after arriving here. As soon as the helicopter landed, myself, other doctors, and the trauma team went to work immediately. We started on him as soon as he was handed to us on the roof of the hospital. He was a strong young man and fought determinedly to save his own life."

By this time Cody's mother, and girlfriend were basket cases, weeping their hearts out, tears gushing out, in the emergency room. Cody's stepfather tried to keep a stoic look on his face, but his emotions succumbed to the tragic news, and he began to sway on his feet.

The doctor held his ground, staring down at the floor. He had been through this ordeal many times and it was taking a toll on his mental stability. Then why did he still practice medicine, he did not know.

"Sit down," the doctor urged them. "Please sit down."

Cody's mother ignored the doctor and asked, "Where is he at? I need to see him."

"Of course," the doctor said. "Please come with me."

Cody's stepfather held his mother up, while his girlfriend held on to Cody's mother's arm.

As they passed rows of curtained areas, they came upon the last one and the doctor said directly to Cody's mother, "Are you ready for this?"

"Yes, I am," she screamed, tears still spilling down her face. "Where's my son?"

Her grief was being replaced with a growing rage. *Who would shoot my son in the back,* she thought. *What a bastard and a coward.* She sensed Cody was unarmed when he was murdered.

Of course, Cody was unarmed. None of those black dudes were going to face him if he was armed. They did not have the courage to face-off with another young man who may kill them.

The doctor pulled the curtains toward him, and Cody's body came into sight. He was covered with a white sheet, from head to toe.

Grieving uncontrollably, Cody's mother removed the sheet from Cody's face. His girlfriend and stepfather gasped in horror. Cody looked as if in a shallow sleep and if touched he might awaken. And his mother wished he would awaken and learn this nightmare was all in her mind.

Cody's mother's grieving was relentless. Cody's girlfriend was stricken with grief. His stepfather appeared as if in a state of shock. He did not know what to do, nor how to console Cody's mother.

She leaned over Cody and kissed him on the face. She took her hand and rubbed it gently across his face. The love for her son was killing her.

Cody's girlfriend kissed him on the face. His stepfather held Cody's hand for a moment.

The doctor was silent. He had seen this many times and it was tearing at his mind.

Cody's mother was now hysterical, grieving beyond grief. Cody's stepfather tried consoling her, but it went nowhere. She was leaning over Cody's body now, telling him how much she loved him, realizing without her son, her life was over. She no longer had anything to live for, nor the will to live.

In a flash of a second her entire life with Cody, from infancy to his death, flashed through her mind. Over and over, she kept reliving how she could have saved her son, had she kept him away from his fake friends who were not friends, but his enemies in disguise.

How right she was!

She was losing her mind and could not control it. If she had a gun in her hand right now, she would probably blow her brains out. That was how much disbelief and grief she was trapped in.

The doctor knew if she could survive the first couple days, she would come to reality that her son was gone, and her life would go on. But the doctor had witnessed many mothers in her position who never made it through the first days and went to the grave with their dead child by grief or suicide.

Cody's girlfriend was mourning almost as much as his mother. The stepfather was slipping deeper into shock.

Without realizing it, another half-hour slipped by, as Cody's mother was hugging him and finally realized it was over for herself and her son. She would never make it without him.

For his mother's sake, the doctor intervened and encouraged her to leave her son. The stepfather and girlfriend practically had to pull Cody's mother away from him.

The doctor told them an autopsy was inevitable. The coroner had to determine all the specifics of the murder, especially where the bullets entered and exited, for the detectives to piece the murder together and collect other vital evidence that could bring the killer to justice.

All three of them tried to console Cody's mother but she was inconsolable.

The doctor pulled the sheet back over Cody's face. Then to the grief of Cody's mother, the doctor closed the curtains.

Cody's mother wept and mourned all the way out of the emergency room. They got into the car and grievingly drove back to Okeechobee.

It was over. Her son was gone. Her life was over.

Cody Clayville, seven years before his death, at age fifteen, was ordered by the court to attend *The Misdemeanor Intervention Program,* for a minor drug offense. If he attended all eight weeks of the program, three times per week, two hours per session, he would not have an offense on his record. It would be wiped off as if it never existed. Upon learning this, he was committed to completing the program.

On the first night he attended the program, Cody met a tiny guy sitting next to him, nicknamed Twitch. Twitch was in the program for a minor theft charge. Twitch was always looking for friends since he had so few. And Cody fit the perfect friend.

Cody was a big guy, tough, bold, took no shit from the punks and mean-muggers. At school he hung with the toughest guys, mainly black, and many of the students, mostly white, avoided him through fear and respect.

Sometimes he would sell Xanax, and Oxycontin, right in school, and show Twitch whatever he had, including Dilaudid for the heroin addicts.

Twitch was one of the few people who wanted to hang out with Cody. Cody and Twitch were a lot alike, and a lot different.

Cody was fair-complected, with dark eyes and hair, appearing to be a mixture of Irish and Latino, a handsome young teenager. Although it appeared Cody was destined to be a criminal, he did not possess the physical attributes of one. Unlike the rugged and raggedy and sleazy appearance of a criminal, he was clean-shaven, friendly, good-hearted, well-spoken, and when he smiled, he exposed a perfect row of shiny-white front teeth. He dressed well and held himself fully upright, as if he came from an upper-middle-class family, which was quite deceiving.

Cody and his mother were living off Sample Road in Coral Springs, a nice neighborhood, but they were kicked out after Cody and his black friend Steve, tossed Cody's safe off the second-floor balcony to break it open, since Cody forgot the combination to the lock.

They made such a ruckus, the nosey neighbors called the Coral Springs police. Cody was just opening the safe when the police arrived. They found money, drugs, and guns inside, and not only did they lose their apartment, Cody was arrested and the contents were seized. Cody never recovered his loss, but did evade the charges, through The Misdemeanor intervention Program.

Cody's mother found another apartment located in Lauderhill, aka, *Deepside,* a filthy crime-ridden black neighborhood, one of the toughest hoods in all of Fort Lauderdale, the only place available and affordable due to overcrowded Broward County.

Due to the low intellect of the people who lived in Deepside, they were so proud of their shithole, they even used the numbers 5519 to represent their hood. The average educational level of these people was between kindergarten and first grade. If a resident of Deepside, male or female, young or old, could correctly recite their ABCs, they were considered educated and stuck out from the others.

Cody was naturally street-smart, ghetto-smart, mingled well with the Blacks in Deepside, and they all respected him. And it was good they respected him, because he would fight, with or without his 9mm pistol, in a fraction of a second, regardless if these people were infamous for being the toughest badass dudes in the world. Without their weapons, they were shit.

Cody only asked, if you wanted a piece of his ass, just to approach him face-to-face, man-to-man. But it was falling on deaf ears. The world today was full of cowards who were too sissified to face another man head-on. So, he made it a point to watch his back at all times.

Cody knew so much about life, he appeared to be much older than his age, although he did look like a teenager.

Cody walked through Deepside as if he owned it. No matter how dangerous it got, he always managed to watch his back. Surprisingly, him and his mother quickly adjusted, and soon the area no longer seemed overly dangerous and depressing.

In Deepside, Cody was selling out of his apartment: heroin, fentanyl, crack, meth, and was competing with other dealers in the building who would usually kill over their turf, but strangely they left Cody alone. Cody was only fifteen years old and standing up to Blacks twice his age and size.

One day Twitch went to Deepside to visit Cody and upon entering the apartment, Twitch immediately noticed the screened-in porch, which had an aluminum sheet covering the lower section of it, had about a dozen perfectly round holes in it.

"What are those holes?" Twitch asked.

"Those are bullet holes," Cody said. "I shoot my gun from inside the house through the aluminum on the balcony, toward the little lake downstairs."

"Are you serious?" Twitch asked. "Do they call the police?"

"Man, no one calls the police here," Cody explained. "We're in the hood."

Cody was quite wild in his early years. Twitch just stared at Cody in awe.

Cody's mother came home shortly after Twitch arrived. She went to her room after Cody introduced Twitch to his mother.

Twitch and Cody went into his bedroom and talked about how rough and dangerous the neighborhood was. Cody then proceeded to take out his guns to show Twitch. Twitch was impressed. Cody was armed to the teeth. He could hold off an army if he had to. Twitch was not easily influenced but with Cody he was.

Cody took hold of his 9mm and pulled the hammer back. It made a clicking sound loud enough to get his mother's attention.

"Cody," she called, sounding alarmed. She was terrified, him or Twitch may accidentally get shot.

"Just showing Twitch my guns, Mom," Cody responded. "Everything's okay."

"Please be careful, Cody!"

"Okay, Mom."

As evening approached Twitch had to go home. The next day Cody seen him, he was smiling and immediately came to the point.

"My Mom doesn't like you, man."

"Really," Twitch said. "I wonder why."

"It's a lot of things," Cody said, still smiling. "It's nothing personal. She doesn't like a lot of people I hang with. I can tell by the way she talks, she's afraid me and you together might get into trouble, especially since I have guns."

"Maybe she thinks I'm influencing you, instead of you influencing me," Twitch smiled.

"Could be." Cody laughed then continued smiling. "I'll only bring you over when she's not around."

"Okay," Twitch said.

On another day, Cody walked down Woodside Drive toward Twitch's house, smoking dope and firing his gun in the air while videotaping it with his cell phone. When he reached Twitch's place, he laughingly showed Twitch the video. Twitch laughed along, realizing Cody was more brazen than the allegedly tough guys in the neighborhood. Cody and Twitch were both surprised nobody had even called the police.

Twitch went as far as telling his father what Cody had done. Instead of being impressed, his father was alarmed. He encouraged Twitch to stop hanging with Cody, for fear they both might end up in jail.

Twitch downplayed it to the best he could to pacify his father. He told his father regardless how wild Cody appeared, that at the end of the day he had a heart of gold, would never hurt anybody unless they bothered him. He would act like he did not have a good heart, but he did. He just was not going to let anybody take advantage of him.

Upon hearing this, it impressed his father, and eased his worries.

About a week later, Twitch and his father were out for the day when Cody called Twitch. Twitch told Cody it would be later in the day before they got home. Cody said he would wait for him. A half-day later Twitch and his father got home and there was Cody sitting on the steps of the stairway. Both Twitch and his father were a little puzzled. Was Cody waiting since morning for Twitch?

Twitch walked up to Cody as his father said hello and went upstairs to their condo.

After conversing a while, Cody and Twitch decided to meet up later that evening. Twitch went upstairs and his father was waiting for the news but decided to speak first.

"I still don't know if it's a good idea to hang with Cody. I know you said he was a good guy, but he seems a little dangerous, son."

"Dad, Cody's been waiting for me all day. He got here at ten and it's five now. That should tell you something about him."

"Yeah, you do have a point there. He must really think a lot of you."

"It's more than that. He's a real friend. A person I can trust and depend on. He would always have my back in case danger ever comes our way. That's a lot more than I can say for my other friends."

"Yeah," his father said. "I have to agree on that. Just be careful when you are with him."

Twitch went on to tell his father what him and Cody were talking about. Cody had confidence in Twitch and trusted his loyalty. He confided in Twitch a lot and Twitch was flattered. Twitch was Cody's most trusted confidant.

He said Cody was an extremely lonely guy. He told Twitch he had no brothers or sisters but did have half-siblings who wanted nothing to do with him. He claimed to have a black girlfriend who was pregnant, possibly with his baby, but there was no proof and she always avoided him. Other than his mother and Aunt Shayne, he had nobody. He was all alone. Cody found it scary and depressing.

Twitch continued explaining to his father that he and Cody had a lot in common. They both experienced a rough life. Both were adventurous and daring. Both had a lot of acquaintances but few friends. Both were very confident but had a slight doubt of their success in life.

And Cody was an only child, just like Twitch and they often discussed this with each other, regarding how lonely and disheartening it was not to have siblings.

As time passed both just accepted it as part of their life. There was nothing they could do about it anyways. Twitch was unsure why Cody had no siblings but for him, it was because the marriage between his mother and father failed. And that ended all chances of siblings, because his father never married again, and his mother was too old.

His father realized Twitch understood Cody well since he was in a similar situation. But he kept it to himself so as not to make Twitch's situation worse.

He told his father Cody once called his father *dad* and his father said, *please don't call me that again.*

Twitch's father shook his head in dismay, "That's not a nice thing to say, especially when Cody has nobody else. I would have never said that."

"Of course, you would have never said that. You wouldn't want to disappoint Cody."

Twitch could see his father was relenting with him hanging with Cody and that was a good thing. Cody had a lot to offer, and Twitch was happy and had a lot to learn.

At this stage of their friendship Cody was the dominant figure. He knew Twitch was a true friend and elevated their friendship.

Twitch finished *The Misdemeanor Intervention Program,* a few weeks before Cody. Cody for unknown reasons missed a few sessions. But they secured their friendship the first night they met.

Cody taught Twitch a lot of things that involved survival. He knew all the ins-and-outs of ghetto life. In the coming months and years, Cody mentored Twitch on the skills of drug-dealing, who he should and should not sell to, how to avoid robberies, how to avoid killings, how to handle his licks, users, and plugs. He mentored Twitch on carrying and using a gun and avoiding the police.

Surprisingly, Twitch excelled in the use of firearms, from his Glock 9mms to his short- and long-barreled Ak47s. He was a natural with guns, and in a short time he became nearly an expert shooter, outperforming the entire neighborhood, possibly even Cody.

Twitch fully absorbed Cody's firsthand lecturing. And Cody was impressed Twitch was a fast learner.

Then Twitch built upon the knowledge and kept safe and alive as his life moved on.

Within a few years Twitch became as tough and skilled as Cody, not physically tough, because he was a small guy anyways, but mentally and spiritually tough. He was as street-smart as Cody now, could slip in and out of dangerous situations unharmed. It turned out both him and Cody were naturally ghetto intelligent, although neither grew up in the ghetto.

As time moved on, Twitch would always confide in his father with everything in his life. On several occasions, Twitch told him that Cody repeated to him on numerous times, he felt he was not going to live much longer. He felt something out of his control was going to cut short his life, as if he was going to be murdered.

Twitch's father's response was that Cody should change his life a little, like stop jacking drug dealers at gunpoint. If anything was going to threaten his life it was that. It was dangerous. The drug dealers had connections as well as Cody. It turned out Cody thought nothing of it, but did stop robbing them, and stayed to himself and sold drugs on his own. Other than that, he did not see why Cody would not live a long life.

Twitch's father again tried to talk Twitch into not hanging with Cody, and it worked for a good while, but unknowingly to his father, Twitch was staying in touch with Cody by phone. Twitch finally broke the news to his father that him and Cody often talked about their dreams, goals and accomplishments in life, how to reach them and how to make something of themselves they could be proud of and leave behind all the fools and losers. His father liked Cody anyways and did not try to discourage Twitch from talking to him.

Once Twitch's father was in Publix on Wiles Road and when he turned, he seen Cody with his backpack on and moving away as if trying to avoid him. He realized that Twitch had informed Cody of his worry of them being together. To relax Cody, he acted as if he did not see Cody, and all was well.

Then one day, to Twitch's father's delight, Twitch told him Cody had moved to the City of Okeechobee and had called him in a very cheerful tone that he no longer felt he was going to die soon and believed he was going to make it through life and make something of himself.

Twitch listened intently but did not quite understand Cody's sudden change in heart. Afterwards, Twitch was happy and so was his father. Cody was suddenly looking at life in a positive perspective. He was even working at Home Depot.

"Come see me work," Cody told Twitch numerous times and Twitch would always say okay, but since Cody was now living in Okeechobee, it was a long drive from Broward County, so Twitch never visited him. He even told Twitch, "Selling drugs is a waste of time. You could make more money working an honest job."

Upon hearing the news, Twitch's father was ecstatic. He hoped Twitch would follow in Cody's footsteps.

After that, Cody was relentless. He would call Twitch periodically and still encourage Twitch to come visit him at Home Depot and see him work. Cody told him he was in charge of a department, and Twitch was impressed. Cody seemed unusually happy, and Twitch said he would visit him, but he still never showed up since Okeechobee was about two hours away.

One evening Cody called and as usual Twitch was happy to hear from him and apologized to Cody for not visiting him at his job.

"Twitch," Cody said, sounding overly excited and repeated what he told Twitch earlier. "I think I'm going to make it in life. I feel good about myself. I'm happy. Life is going good for me. I have an apartment. I have a job. I've been with my girlfriend for four years. I was always concerned I would be murdered in crime-ridden Broward County but not anymore. . ."

Twitch stayed silent, happy for Cody, letting Cody do all the talking. He knew Cody had a few run-ins with the law in the past, and it may have temporarily hurt his confidence, his self-esteem. But that was all in the past now, because it appeared Cody had overcome it all.

"Twitch," Cody continued excitedly. "I bet when we are in our forties, we will still be in touch. We're going to be friends for life."

"I think we will," Twitch finally said.

Cody had slowed down now. He was giving Twitch the chance to talk.

"That makes me happy for both of us," Twitch said.

"Yeah, that will be great," Cody said.

As time passed Cody was still living in Okeechobee holding the same job at Home Depot, but as inflation grew and Cody's salary stayed the same, his expenses soon exceeded his pay. Cody had no other alternative than to revert back to dealing. How else could he pay his rent? Pay his bills? But he was a bit older now and a lot wiser and only dealt with marijuana.

He would commute to Broward County, visit a plug, a dealer, he knew well and who highly liked Cody, pick up a pound for a phenomenal price, then resell it by the ounces and Twitch was the first one he would contact. Almost always Twitch would purchase a couple ounces from Cody, though periodically, Twitch would take a raincheck until Cody showed up again and he was running low on stock.

Twitch always told his father there was no one in Broward who had the best contacts and buyers than Cody. Cody had the innate gift of *networking,* of making connections and building business relationships, as well as making friends with the biggest dealers and he was always respected by the dealers. Cody was even able to build contacts with the worse of the plugs, that nobody else wanted to deal with. He somehow befriended them, and they befriended him. The best and worst plugs were always happy to see Cody show up, even when Cody took merchandise on credit on numerous occasions and could not pay it back right away. They never became angry with Cody and their respect and friendship with Cody remained intact.

Cody commuting back and forth to Broward continued for a long time. Then one day Cody contacted Twitch and mentioned he would like to return to Broward to live. Twitch tried to discourage Cody for his own good, by telling him why would he want to come back to this cesspool? Broward County was as bad as Miami now, the dumping grounds of all the sewage from around the world. Cody listened to Twitch but was not deterred. Before Twitch or anyone else realized it, Cody was living with his girlfriend in Pompano.

Twitch had few friends, two half-siblings who wanted nothing to do with him, and was as lonely as Cody, if not more, but did have many associates, none of which he could trust. But hanging with them was better than nothing. At least he would not be isolated from the world. To Twitch, living his life alone was tantamount to a nightmare. Many of his associates tried to befriend Twitch, but instinct prodded him to keep his distance.

Twitch had to control his associates since most of them were his licks, purchasing his products, and business was decent. He knew if he gave them the chance, they would rip him off without a second thought then go around the neighborhood boasting they had ripped off Twitch. Twitch had a growing reputation around the neighborhood, though he was still trailing Cody's, and was not going to let these punks tarnish his image. He did not want to have to bust open their heads, so to avoid violence, he put restrictions on them, and it worked. But, as a courtesy, he did let many of them hang around his crib after they purchased.

Twitch's two main associates were George, a stoned Mexican, and Kelley, a sly-dealing Haitian. Kelley was much better than George, especially in friendship and honesty and intelligence. George was abnormally treacherous, just a true snake slithering in the dark, who would lie, cheat, steal and rip-off his own so-called friends.

So eventually Twitch began to hang with only Kelley as he needed friendship and company so he would not be stressed all the time.

Although Cody lived close by now, Twitch rarely seen much of him. So instead of being alone, he finally allowed George to hang around his crib as much as he wanted, especially since George was one of his best licks, spending almost all his money on products. Twitch believed George could be a good guy, but it was a hard feat to accomplish so George took the easiest route and stayed bad.

To complicate matters further, George was a perpetually stoned troublemaker, a replica of a street punk. For all the years, Twitch knew him, he was never sober, taking any type of drug, from smoking marijuana to shooting opiates and heroine. He always tried to coerce others to do dope with him, but everybody refused.

That was when George turned to his black girlfriends into shooting dope with him. Sometimes it worked. Most of the times it did not. Even his girlfriends, after getting to know him, seemed to shy away from him.

George loved to show off and was always looking for attention, especially from his few friends. He would speed dangerously down the streets where kids were playing ball, never once concerned he might run one over, repeatedly revving his engine to a loud roar and looking around smiling as people got out of his way, his mop of black hair blowing in the wind, hoping someone, anyone, would notice him.

But it was futile. Other than Twitch and Kelley, nobody wanted anything to do with him, much less notice him. He could not be trusted, and everybody knew it. George constantly had a lit joint in his hand and a dumb smile on his face that never went away. They could tell he was a man by age but a child in mind and avoided him.

George would take puff after puff on his joint and the dumb smile on his face would turn into a moronic grin as the marijuana thrust him into a world of all his own.

He would shoot his guns in the air without a care of endangering anybody. Still, other than Twitch and Kelley, nobody ever noticed him. He had to find a way to get the attention he needed. Being unnoticed, was driving him nuts. George was unable to realize, he was already nuts. Drugs had eaten away his brains.

During Cody's absence, Twitch and Kelley began to develop a friendship. Twitch's father even started taking a liking to Kelley, which was unusual because he usually did not like anybody Twitch hung with.

Then one day strangely Kelley suddenly disappeared, and Twitch and his father did not even notice it until after a few weeks.

"What happened to Kelley?" his father asked.

"I wish I knew," Twitch said.

"Maybe he got tired of coming around."

"I don't think so, Dad," Twitch said, looking concerned. "I think he could be in jail."

"Really?" his father said.

"I'm going to find out," Twitch said.

A few days later, Twitch approached his father and showed him a website he went on that listed all the people arrested in Broward County. And sure enough, there was Kelley's mugshot with a short description of his arrest and charges.

"I knew it was over drugs," Twitch said. "They got him for sale of crack cocaine."

"Well, he knew of the severity of his crime before he got arrested," his father said. "I sure hope he gets a lenient sentence."

"He probably will," Twitch said. "It's his first arrest and felony charge."

Twitch began to reread the description of the charge. "Oh, and they got him for possession of marijuana. Just a minor charge. Marijuana is almost legal now."

"That's nice to hear," his father said. "You want to go see him in jail?"

"I'm not sure if that's a good idea," Twitch said. "They record visitor conversations, and he might not want us there. It could be more of a problem for him if he or we say the wrong thing. And you sure don't want to discuss his charges with him. They might record something they can use against him."

"You're absolutely right. I should have thought about that myself."

"Don't worry, Dad. If I get more news, I'll let you know."

As the first month moved on, Twitch would intermittently find additional news of Kelly's case and would often discuss it with his father.

"Can you imagine it's been two months now and Kelley has not even went to trial," Twitch said, surprised.

His father was just as surprised since Kelley's charges were not so serious.

"From what I've heard, they can keep you indefinitely before giving you a trial. Also, I heard that sometimes they keep the offender in jail so long that when they do go to court, the judge gives them time served."

"Yeah, that's fairly common, Dad."

"Oh, I didn't know that."

"I'll keep tabs on Kelley and let you know if anything new comes up."

Surprisingly, Kelley still did not show up after another month passed but Twitch had been following his case religiously and learned that Kelley had been placed in the stockade and would soon be released.

His father was pleased to hear the good news and shortly after they both stopped discussing Kelley's situation since they expected him to be released any day now.

But it took another month before Kelley was finally released.

Twitch explained to his father that Kelley's parents went back to Haiti for a couple months and Kelley had nowhere to go but on the streets. Twitch's father did not want Kelley on the streets, so he told Twitch to bring Kelley here. If he lived on the streets, he would be in trouble again. It would be a disaster if Kelley ended up back in jail. He might not be so lucky to be released again after a couple months.

Twitch was happy his father accepted Kelley into their household.

After Kelley lived with them for a couple months, he offered Twitch's father rent money, but he refused it. Kelley needed the money more than him. Kelley kept silent and put the money back in his pocket.

After a few more months it was as if Kelley became part of the family. His father looked at Kelley now as his own son. Twitch, Kelley and his father would sit up late at night discussing all the events in the neighborhood.

Then late one night after Kelley came home and him and Twitch were watching TV, a loud knock came to the door and Twitch yelled out, "Who is it?"

"The police."

The police? What did they want?

"Just a moment," Twitch yelled. He then hurried to his father's bedroom and explained that the police were knocking on the door.

His father just stared at him as he lay in bed. His father was not a police-lover and told Twitch he would handle it.

As his father idled the police began knocking again but he would not answer the door. The knocking got louder. The knocking got rhythmic.

Bang! Bang! Bang!

His father just stood in the living room with Twitch and Kelley.

He would not answer the door and the police would not stop banging.

"What's going on, Dad?"

"That's what I would like to know. Did you do something?"

"No, Kelley walked in and ten minutes later the police were at the door."

Bang! Bang! Bang!

The police would not relent, and neither would his father.

"Answer the door, Dad. We didn't do nothing."

Kelley chimed in, "Answer the door we don't have nothing to hide. We didn't do nothing wrong."

"If the police want in that bad let them break down the door, then," his father asserted.

His father turned to Kelley. "Were the police after you when you came here?"

"No, not at all. There was nobody outside who seen me come in."

"Do you have anything on you?"

"No, nothing."

"Then the neighbors must have called the police," his father said.

"They might break down the door, Dad," Twitch said nervously.

"Then let them break down the door. I'm not going to make it easy on them and open it."

Twitch and Kelley both were nervous and still wanted to open the door, but his father would not comply.

As the banging on the door continued both Kelley and Twitch kept telling his father to open the door, but he still refused. The police were not going to push him around.

Bang! Bang! Bang!

The banging went on for another ten minutes then ceased. The police gave up, which proved to his father they were just being harassed. He explained it to Twitch so he would not think his father was committing a crime. He did not want Twitch to ever oppose the police since he already taught Twitch to have a high respect for authority.

But to be on the safe side, he told Twitch to tell Kelley not to come by anymore until they found out what this was all about.

Kelley was not happy to leave but immediately complied.

After this incident Twitch told his father on numerous occasions, he learned something invaluable. Never answer the door for the police if you did nothing wrong.

Twitch's father never let Kelley come back to live with them but still fostered a family friendship with him. Kelly showed up all the time and at all times of the day or night. His father was pleased he kept a good friendship with Twitch. He still looked at Kelley as a son.

Kelley spent so much time with them that it suddenly dawned on his father that Kelley appeared to have no friends other than Twitch. He was concerned for Kelley. Kelley was living a secluded life. No family? No friends?

He approached Twitch, "Son, doesn't Kelley have other friends?"

"He's got plenty of friends around here but rarely deals with them. The problem is he cannot trust any of them. They have ripped him off at times and he never mentioned it to them, just stopped going around them." Twitch hesitated with a smile. "I'm the only friend he can trust and the only true friend he has."

"That explains everything," his father said and dropped the subject.

About four years preceding Cody's death, when he and Twitch boasted a fantastic friendship, he showed up one day at Twitch's condo to pay a visit. Twitch was ecstatic to see him and reluctantly introduced Cody to Kelley. Cody noticed Twitch's reluctance to introduce the two but kept it to himself.

It was not that he did not want Cody and Kelley to form a friendship, but it appeared to Twitch there was a vast difference of the types of intelligence levels between the two. But at first introduction Cody was diplomatic and smiled and shook hands. Although they became friends, it was a couple years before Cody and Kelley actually began to hang out.

A couple weeks later, Cody unexpectedly showed up again at Twitch's condo, wearing a black backpack. This time one of Twitch's licks was there riding through his high. It was George, but Twitch was not about to introduce Cody to him. George was not Twitch's friend, just a purchaser, and Twitch tolerated him and allowed George to relax at his crib while he was high, instead of driving off and getting involved in an automobile accident.

"Hey, Cody, nice to see you," Twitch said. "You should have called first to be sure I was home."

"And if I did miss you, I would have met up with you later, anyways," Cody said.

"So what's up?" Twitch asked.

"Nothing much," Cody said. "If you need anything, I got a few things to show you."

"I'm okay, now," Twitch said. "Thanks anyways. I'll let you know when I need something."

Cody hung around for a while, talked to George a little, but most of all just chatted with Twitch.

George suddenly got up to leave, said goodbye to them both, then walked out.

As soon as George shut the door, Twitch looked at Cody and smiled.

"Nice to see George leave. I didn't want him to know I purchase from you once in a while. I just don't trust that George."

"I don't blame you," Cody said. "I don't trust anybody these days."

"Anyways, show me what you got."

Cody took off his backpack unzipped it and took a seat next to Twitch. He brought out a bundle of fresh, crisp ounces of marijuana. He opened the plastic bag and handed it to Twitch, and the aroma instantly filled the room.

"Here, take a deep whiff of this." Cody was smiling because he knew Twitch was already approving its quality.

Twitch, with a serious look on his face said, "I don't have to check it out. I can already tell its top quality."

Cody smelled it and Twitch finally took a whiff too. They bargained over the prices for a while. Twitch had a serious look on his face. When they bought and sold among each other, it was as if they were not friends, just serious merchants.

Twitch was dithering over the prices. He felt Cody's prices was a little high but reasoned that at least he was getting good quality weed.

"I'll take a couple ounces," Twitch said.

"Take it all," Cody encouraged. He did not want to drive around Coral Springs, looking for other buyers. He needed to get home to his girlfriend, so she would not get angry he had taken too long. "I'll give you the whole QP for four hundred. That's a great price."

"Okay," Twitch assented. "I'll take it. It is a good deal."

Twitch got on hands and knees and put his hand underneath the couch. First, he pulled out a 9mm pistol. Then he fumbled around a few seconds until he felt his wad of hundred-dollar bills. He pulled out the money and took off the rubber band, then handed four of the bills to Cody.

Cody said nothing while putting the money in his pocket, his eyes focusing on the 9mm.

"It's good you don't take any chances," Cody said, smiling. "I do the same thing. I keep my piece within reach all the time."

"You got to," Twitch said. "I don't always like it but I have no other choice. Nobody can be trusted anymore, especially when drugs are involved."

"Yeah, that's the truth," Cody said.

Twitch's father walked out of the bedroom, said hello to Cody, and walked out the door. When he got outside, he saw a group of police cars close to his car and the police were walking to an apartment on the first floor. His first response was to call Twitch and warn him and Cody. But he had to drive off first so the police would not notice him.

By the time he was dialing the number, Cody and Twitch had wrapped up their deal and Cody was out the door, and Twitch, as usual, locked the door behind him. Cody had other drugs in his backpack, mainly hard drugs.

When Twitch did not answer his phone, his father hung up and called again.

By this time, Twitch got the biggest surprise he had had in a long time. There was loud banging on the door. Twitch looked out the peephole and seen it was Cody. He was startled, confused, and slowly opened the door. Cody tried to rush inside but Twitch instinctively held the door shut, more confused.

"Crackas," Cody blurted. "Crackas. Crackas outside."

Twitch was in a mild panic. Crackas meant police. What was Cody doing? Where were the police?

Twitch still held the door shut. Cody, by this time, was trying to force his way into the apartment. But Twitch held it partially shut, assuming the police were about to descend upon them. When he finally noticed the police were not behind Cody, he let Cody in.

Cody seemed to be in a panic. Once inside his panic began to subside. He explained to Twitch what happened. He saw the police as he was walking on the second floor and thought they were on their way up. As they both were looking out the peephole, they realized the police had gone elsewhere and now they were driving off. It was a scare for both of them.

Cody finally got in his car and cranked the engine, in relief. Had he gotten busted again, he would have gotten a long sentence in jail. He could not let that happen.

As Cody started driving off, Twitch's father was pulling into the parking lot and was glad to see the police gone. He tried to get Cody to stop by waving at him, but Cody kept driving away.

He went upstairs and Twitch recounted the story for him.

His father was upset and again urged Twitch to stop hanging with Cody. It fell on deaf ears. Cody was his plug. Cody had contact with every plug in Broward County and still making connections.

His father broke the news to Twitch, that he had been trying to call him and warn him and Cody about the police, but Twitch did not answer the phone.

"I was so busy with Cody, I didn't realize you were calling," Twitch explained. "Next time I'll be more attentive."

"I hope so," his father explained. "Had you picked up the phone you could have warned Cody to stay in the condo until the police left."

"It won't happen again," Twitch promised. "Could you imagine if the police were chasing after Cody, and he ran inside here. They could have legally broken down the door. We both would have been busted. It would have been all Cody's fault for coming back to the apartment."

"Forget about putting blame on him," his father said. "Just be thankful things worked out in you and Cody's favor. You both are plugs and the police would have been delighted to get two plugs in one bust."

"I'll talk with Cody about being more careful, Dad."

"It's imperative you do. No reason for either of you to get busted."

A couple months passed, and Twitch had not heard from Cody but did not mention it to his father. Surprisingly, one day, late at night, Cody called Twitch. Twitch was euphoric to hear from Cody.

He learned Cody had been in jail and was unable to contact him. Cody promised to see Twitch the next day. Twitch could not wait for Cody to arrive and could not wait to tell his father. He hurried to his bedroom.

"Dad," Twitch blurted. "Cody just called. He's been in jail. That's why we haven't heard from him for a couple months."

"If we had known we could have visited him in jail," his father said. "Probably nobody came to visit him."

"I'm the first one he called as soon as he got out of jail." Twitch was elated and flattered.

"He thinks a lot of you," he said. "What was he in jail for?"

"Who knows? He didn't tell me, and I didn't ask. Probably got busted for drugs like everybody else."

"That sounds right. Let's hope he stays out of jail."

The very next day, Cody showed up and Twitch and his father both were excited to see Cody. After Cody and Twitch got caught up on the last couple months events, it was as if they got reacquainted.

Twitch quickly employed Cody's services and easily got rid of some stuff with a single transaction. Twitch was pleased. Cody then asked Twitch for a loan and Twitch instinctively said no, but instantly recanted with a smile as he noticed Cody's temper rising. His father even intervened and reminded Twitch Cody just helped him and to give Cody money whenever he needed it as a sign of appreciation and friendship.

Cody came out of jail broke and needed to get restarted on making money. Twitch gave Cody some cash and an ounce of weed. Cody walked out of the condo and within thirty minutes came back with his pocket full of money.

Twitch's father pulled Twitch aside, "How did he get rid of that stuff so fast?"

"Dad, everybody around here knows him, and he walks down the street advertising his inventory loudly without worrying or caring if the police see him. His friends come out and purchase and make conversation with him, especially when he's been gone for a while. They all look up to Cody."

"Why did you refuse Cody when he asked for some money to get restarted and he made that deal for you and didn't get a cent out of it? He did it as a favor to you."

"I know. I always say no at first when anybody asks for money. But I would have given it to Cody anyways. I would never refuse Cody a loan."

"Whenever he wants a loan be sure to give it to him."

"Of course, Dad. I wouldn't think twice."

Cody handed Twitch a handful of cash and paid him off. Cody then purchased more stash from Twitch then had to leave to get back home.

Twitch was still proud he was the first person Cody called upon his release from jail.

Within a week Cody was back as he asked Twitch for another loan and Twitch happily complied. Cody paid him back within a couple days.

Cody did not come around again for a long time. As the months passed Cody did stay in touch with Twitch by phone.

One day George called Twitch for an ounce of marijuana, and him and his friend Darius came by and picked it up and sent Twitch a fake PayPal payment. Before Twitch caught the rip off, George and Darius again called for another ounce, and this time only George picked up the weed, and again sent a fake PayPal payment, totaling over eight-hundred-dollars. It took about another hour before the rip off showed up in Twitch's account.

Twitch called George and Darius and Darius was the spokesman. He explained to Twitch he was very sorry over the so-called bad PayPal transaction, but claimed he also lost money, and they had to go down in a loss together. Twitch knew he was lying and was angry but left it at that. He would deal with Darius later.

Finally, George had gotten his chance to rip off Twitch and Twitch immediately dumped him as a lick, but first had the urge to bust open George's face with a hammer, but knew it was useless. Even with a busted face, George would never learn a lesson, because he was too addicted to drugs. So, Twitch just let him go and stopped serving him.

Twitch told his father and both of them were angry. They both had treated George fairly and that was a good enough reason to be angry.

When Twitch's other friends heard he ripped off Twitch they were in disbelief. So now, George's few associates began to avoid him, but George was relentless; he would ceaselessly call them to come over, lie and connive that he too lost money in the transaction due to an error in PayPal, and swear of his innocence, hoping to make them believe he never ripped off Twitch.

When Twitch heard this, he laughed and claimed George would be dead in an instant if he ripped off the Blacks.

But George's associates all knew better. George became an outcast in the neighborhood. Only his druggie friend Darius stayed by his side.

Kelley had been serving George as well and never had a reason to disassociate himself with George, especially since George had slyly convinced Kelley that Twitch no longer liked him and made up all kinds of false accusations against him. Kelley had so few friends and desperate to have more, bought the story that had so many holes in it, a moron could see George was lying.

Eventually Kelley fell even deeper into George's trap and unhesitatingly ate up the continuous lies he made about Twitch and began to hang with George every day. When Kelly's friends and Twitch learned he was hanging with George, they knew he lost his mind and stopped hanging with Kelley. And as time passed, it seemed as if George and Kelley had no other friends but themselves. Not only did they hang out alone, but it seemed like nobody wanted anything to do with either of them now.

Originally George had been Kelley's lick but from what they could conceive, George had furtively dominated Kelley and was now the boss and was corrupting Kelley, although Kelley was twenty-five with some brains and George twenty with no brains, and Kelley should have known better than to let a moron take control of him. But strange things happen all the time.

Twitch asked Kelley many times, why he was hanging with that moron George, but Kelley would get angry and say George was not a moron, even though he knew George was. Kelley never made any other remark. George was Kelley's only friend now.

From that moment on, Twitch wanted nothing to do with Kelley. He was insulting Twitch's intelligence.

Even Twitch's father was laughing at Kelley. George, a borderline idiot, calling the shots was funny. Kelley was slipping out of reality. Twitch's father was looking at Kelly differently now. He was wondering if he made a mistake regarding Kelley as his son.

About a month later, Kelley called Twitch and asked him to go to a party with him and George and Twitch refused on the spot. He still wanted nothing to do with George and wanted little to do with Kelley. But Kelley's calls kept coming relentlessly, incessantly badgering Twitch. Finally, Twitch succumbed to Kelley's calls and agreed like a fool, but made it unequivocally clear he was only going for Kelley.

They arrived at a party where Twitch was unfamiliar with all the people there. Twitch kept a close watch on George, knowing he loved to start fights then when getting beat up he would depend on his friends to save him and sometimes like idiots, they would. He was skillful at suckering people into dangerous situations, especially to do his fighting for him. He was also a born troublemaker and had no respect for his friends.

And tonight, was no exception. Within minutes George started his screaming and shouting expletives to build his courage. It did not appear he had singled anybody out, just wanted to cause trouble and finally his courage began to rise. By this time the partygoers wanted him out and began to call his bluff as they approached him. Before anybody realized it, the party had turned into a riot.

Twitch realized they were lucky. They were at an all-white middle-class party where people were not as violent and more educated than street punks.

Twitch turned to make his escape and saw two guys had George cornered and were pounding him in the head, rattling his brains, trying to knock some sense into him. Then before Twitch realized what was happening, a whole group of people were beating on George. Twitch had to help. He hated to do it but he had to.

He ran up and punched the biggest guy in the chest to get him off George. The big guy stopped in his tracks and took a deep gasp as if about to collapse. Then Kelley ran up and started fighting to save George as they were outnumbered and had to get out of there. Finally, they fought their way out and made it to the car with the partygoers close behind. Suddenly they were trapped again, surrounded, unable to drive off as the people were trying to pull them out of the car.

"Drive," Twitch hollered. "Drive."

"We're blocked in," Kelley hollered back.

"Force your way through," Twitch urged.

"Hurry up," George yelled. "They're going to kill us."

George was terrified and despite the dangerous position they were in, Twitch had an urge to laugh but held back.

Finally, the car lurched forward, plowing into a few people, knocking everybody else out of the way, then roared off into the night. It was a close call. Middle-class or not they all could have been killed. Those partygoers were angry.

Afterwards, George boasted of beating up the whole crowd by himself. Twitch and Kelley were just happy to get away unscathed. They both knew George was trying to impress them and to delude himself into believing he really took on the whole crowd by himself. It was childish but dangerous. They could have easily been killed. Had they been fighting illiterate street punks they would have never gotten out alive.

Twitch vowed to never go anywhere with them again. George was either going to get himself or somebody else killed.

As the fool George proved he was, Kelley continued to hang with him.

Afterwards, Twitch took a close look at the situation and wondered how he was dumb enough to get suckered into going to the party. It was his own fault. He was trying to please Kelley. If this was all there was to life, he dreaded the future. Then it dawned on him, life was what you made of it. He would never make the same mistake twice.

When his father heard the news, he was disgusted and disgruntled and told Twitch to take George to Liberty City to let the Blacks kill him. They would be doing the world a favor.

A couple weeks afterwards, Cody paid Twitch an unexpected visit at his condo. He was with Kelley and Twitch was so happy to see them both. He had not seen Cody in months. All three were in the parking lot talking about everything and anything but what confused Twitch was that he was hanging with Kelley, something he never expected, mainly because Cody and Kelley seemed to have nothing in common. He slightly regretted introducing Cody to Kelley and George, but never thought Cody would actually hang out with them.

Twitch vetted the situation profoundly. The more he analyzed, the more he concluded that both George and Kelley were definitely out of place with Cody. At first Twitch could not pinpoint why but could just feel it. After heavy assessment, it finally dawned on Twitch. He realized Cody was too intelligent to be hanging with dudes with marginal intelligence. But if that was what Cody wanted, then that was what Cody would do. Nobody could make Cody's decisions for him.

After a few minutes, Twitch's father conversed with them too. He was also happy to see Cody, because Cody had started hanging with Twitch when he was fifteen and he took a liking to Cody. At times when Twitch was in school Cody would sit on the benches in front of the office waiting hours for Twitch to get out of class.

Twitch's father was bemuddled. Twitch and Cody both attended Coral Springs High School and were in the same grade. Why was Cody waiting for Twitch to get out of school instead of attending classes. Twitch's father kept it to himself for a couple days then finally asked Twitch what was going on.

Twitch explained it precisely and tersely. Cody had gotten kicked out of school and was attending a substitute school for problematic students and was leaving class early to meet him.

His father digested the information. He felt bad for Cody and hoped Cody would finish his education.

They continued their conversation for another half-hour. His father pulled Cody aside and apologized to him for Twitch, when he and Twitch had an argument a while back, after Cody jokingly pointed a strong laser beam into Twitch's eyes. Cody had gotten offended by Twitch's rude remarks afterwards and walked out of the condo.

Cody acknowledged the apology with a smile and said it was okay.

Twitch's father was pleased. Would Cody ever hold a grudge against anybody?

Twitch would claim, even years later, that the indelible dot he always sees in his eyes was caused by the laser.

Twitch approached Cody quietly when Kelley started conversing with his father.

"Cody," Twitch said, changing the subject. "What are you doing hanging around with Kelley and George? They don't seem to fit in with you."

"You know me, Twitch. I don't have many friends. I'm always lonely. They're not that bad."

"Yeah, Kelley's okay, but George is like a child."

"They're not that bad," Cody said again.

"Take my advice and dump them both. They're bad news, Cody. They might get you killed. I know you're not going to listen to me, so I wish you the best."

The subject was dropped and after a while they ended their conversation.

As darkness began to descend, Cody decided to leave but promised Twitch he would drop by again soon, as well as stay in touch by phone. Cody and Kelley got in Cody's car and drove off down Woodside Drive, the car's taillights glowing in the descending darkness.

Twitch did not know where they were going but was acutely concerned for Cody's safety.

A few days later, Kelley showed up at Twitch's crib and had some news to give him. Kelley seemed to be in deep thought. Twitch was only imagining what it could be. He never seen Kelley thinking so hard.

"You won't believe it," Kelley started.

Twitch was impatient, eager to hear the news.

"I won't believe what?" Twitch asked.

Kelley blinked his eyes a few times, procrastinating, annoying Twitch.

"Well," Kelley said. "Cody called and I told him to meet me at Marcel's house. Cody shows up and me and Marcel both jumped into Cody's car." Again, Kelley seemed to be thinking harder than usual, still procrastinating, and it was annoying Twitch more.

"Well," Twitch mumbled.

"Well, Cody tells Marcel he can't come with us and Marcel refuses to get out of the car. I can tell Cody's getting mad. He leans over the front seat and opens the door and again tells Marcel he can't come with us and to get out. Marcel still refuses, trying to act bad now. Probably thinking Cody's going to give in and let him come. Then Cody puts his hand under his seat and pulls out his 9mm and points it right at Marcel, then yells, *'get the fuck out.'*".

Twitch began smiling, knowing Cody had a bad temper and did not like Marcel. He claimed Marcel did too much dope and was deceitful and disrespectful.

"Really," Twitch said.

"Really. Marcel looked a little scared. Then gets out of the car."

"Well, at least Marcel isn't stupid. I would of gotten out of the car myself."

"Marcel slams the door and Cody and me drives off. It was over. And I was glad. I didn't say nothing, and Cody didn't say nothing. But I could tell Cody was glad to get rid of Marcel. I don't know what happened between Cody and Marcel."

Twitch was smiling. Cody had a lot of courage. But his father said Cody was too courageous, and that could be dangerous.

"And that's just the beginning," Kelley said.

"Just the beginning?" Twitch said, smiling more.

"We're near the beach driving around looking at the girls when me and Cody start arguing," Kelley said.

"Really? About what?"

"About some nonsense. I don't even remember exactly what it was, but Cody was getting me mad, and finally I said if you want to fight, just pull over."

"Without saying a word, Cody pulls off the road and I get out of the car, thinking he's going to get out and we're going to fight. The next thing I know I see him driving off. He left me on the beach, and I had to catch an Uber home. That was wrong, man."

"Not really," Twitch said. "He's just like me. He doesn't want to fight his friends. He figured it was better to drive off than fight you. He knows the next day you both are going to make up."

"Yeah," Kelley said. "I guess you're right. But truthfully, I don't think I'll ever see him again."

"Why you say that?"

"Cody's got a bad temper."

"Yeah, he does. But you never know," Twitch said. "He just doesn't like his friends challenging him. You should have known better than that. We'll have to wait and see."

Nobody heard from Cody for a long time and Twitch was beginning to wonder if Cody would ever show up. Then one day, unexpectedly, Twitch got a phone call on *WhatsApp,* and it was Cody video calling him. And what a pleasant surprise for Twitch and his father.

Cody's face popped up on the screen, full of enthusiasm and ebullience.

"Twitch, what's up!" Cody practically yelled in good spirits. Cody sounded like he was basking in heaven.

"Where you been, man?"

"Ecuador, man. Way down in Ecuador."

"Ecuador? Where's Ecuador?"

"Come on, man. Ecuador, South America."

"What are you doing there?"

"Visiting relatives with my Mom. It's different down here."

"What do you mean?" Twitch asked.

"Things aren't the same down here, like in Broward County." Cody got right to the point. "It's dangerous, man. It's dangerous. Let me show you around."

Cody focused the phone's video outside the window of the house then zoomed in. Twitch's father stood beside him and began watching the screen with Twitch.

"See down that road where that building is?" Cody said. "A lot of bad people hang out there."

"What's so bad about them?" Twitch asked. "They can't be any worse there than here."

"It's not that they're worse here, man, it's that entire neighborhoods are involved in crime and working together. That's what makes it really bad. You can't trust anybody."

Twitch's father detected danger and immediately intervened. He knew Cody was hardly afraid of anything. And that was not only dangerous, but not smart either. He looked into the camera so Cody could see him.

"Cody, you're not going down in that area by yourself, are you?"

Cody laughed, "No, I'm not allowed. I know better than that. I was told you can get kidnapped and held for ransom."

"Yeah, I've heard that too. And if you can't pay, they sometimes kill you."

"I've heard that too."

Cody started laughing again.

It was obvious in Cody's tone of voice he was in excellent spirits and Twitch's father was happy for him.

"Okay, Cody," he said. "Just wanted to be sure. You got to take care of yourself."

"Of course," Cody still laughed. "Let me show you the rest of the place." Cody moved the phone's camera to another street. "See down that area. It's real poor. I mean people are really poor. That area is infested with drugs and violence. Even the police stay away from that area."

Twitch interrupted as he was laughing. He liked the idea the police were afraid. "Really, man?"

"Yeah, the police are afraid of those people."

Cody and Twitch both laughed together.

Twitch's father was amused but concerned that neither Cody nor Twitch realized the severity of the danger. Maybe they were taking life for granted and felt invulnerable to danger when it stood before them.

Cody commenced showing Twitch around and focused the camera on the inside of his house. The interior walls were painted light green as Cody went from room to room.

"You notice the house is solid concrete. That's because the house has to last a long time for the next generation to live in. Look at the bars on the windows. That just shows how dangerous the area is. You can't trust anybody around here."

Then Cody pointed the camera at the bars on the doors and Twitch's father could not help but comment.

"Cody, when you got bars on the front door, you know it's dangerous."

Cody laughed again. He was getting a kick out of Twitch's father's worries.

"Man, you got bars on everything here."

"That means you can't trust anybody there," Twitch's father said.

"I've already told you that."

"I don't think I would want to live like that."

"Yeah, that can be bad," Cody said. "By the way, they are going to put this house in my name."

"That's nice, Cody. But what good is that going to do if you live in the States and the house is in Ecuador."

"Yeah, you got a point there."

After a few more minutes of Cody showing them how life was in Ecuador his father said goodbye.

"Okay, Cody, I'm going to leave you and Twitch alone. I'll see you when you get back. Take care and be safe, okay?"

"Oh yeah," Cody said. "I'll be okay. See you later."

Cody and Twitch commenced conversing for a good ten minutes nonstop.

Twitch was curious. "Cody, can you serve down there?"

"No, not really," Cody explained. "If you get busted here you can go to jail for a long time, especially if you are a foreigner. And I hear the prisons here are the worst in the world. There's violence in the prison system and the guards let it go on. They can't stop it."

"Wow, that's really bad," Twitch said.

"So how is everybody in Broward?"

"Okay, but you know I don't hang with hardly anybody anymore."

"Yeah, I remember you told me that before."

Their conversation continued for a little longer before they agreed to meet when Cody got back to the States.

They hung up and Twitch and his father began discussing Cody.

"Cody's a hell of a nice guy," his father said. "But I still say his lifestyle brings trouble with it."

"It does, but I hardly hang with him anymore, so I'm not worried about getting in trouble."

That was what his father wanted to hear from Twitch. Cody had been in jail a number of times and that was real concern to him. He did not want Twitch being a cellmate of Cody's.

Cody was a forgiving person, especially to his friends. Kelley had really pissed him off, but he couldn't bring himself to holding grudges, so as soon as he got back from Ecuador, Cody was hanging with Kelley again.

When Twitch learned of this, he refused to answer Kelley's calls, and they were constantly coming in, one after the other. Kelley was still hanging with George, and Twitch wanted nothing to do with either of them.

At Kelley's urging, Cody finally called Twitch.

"We're going to a party. Come with us, Twitch."

"Where's it at?" Twitch asked.

"In Miami."

"Oh, The Boss Mansion. I've been there before. I didn't like it. I'm not going."

"Come on, Twitch. Come with us."

"No. I'm not going. George is always starting fights and getting us to help him fight."

"We won't take George," Cody promised.

"No. I'm not going," Twitch said again. "George will still show up at the party."

"Okay," Cody finally said, and hung up.

Cody and Kelley just drove around the city, contemplating going to the party. Suddenly George called and Cody did not answer the phone. He and Kelley did not want George hanging with them tonight. But George was relentless. He wanted to go to the party with them and called about twenty more times and Cody still did not pick up the phone.

George wanted to go because his black girlfriend decided to go meet some black guys and George knew what that meant. She was going to have sex with them.

George knew that at the party at The Boss Mansion there was always a petite black girl there that he liked and had sex with her before and now he wanted to have sex with her again. It was first come, first serve. So he had to get there quickly, before all those sleazy black dudes got to her first.

Here was his chance to have a good time and get back at his girlfriend. He would teach his girlfriend a lesson. She wanted sex with other guys, and he could show her he could have sex with other girls.

So, George again began calling Cody and Kelley excessively and finally Cody answered the phone. After a long discussion he and Kelley agreed to pick up George.

George was practically out of his mind from drugs, as he climbed into Cody's car, talking nonsense and street gibberish that Cody and Kelley both could hardly understand.

Cody again called Twitch. He liked Twitch and wanted his company.

When Twitch picked up the phone, Cody immediately spoke, "Twitch, come on. Let's all go to the party. We picked up George."

"Cody, stay away from that George. It's a warning. He's bad news. George can't be trusted. He doesn't have our backs as we have his back. Remember last week when I told you that George started a fight at a party and got us all into a fight?"

"Yeah, I remember but there won't be any fighting tonight."

George heard Twitch complaining about him. He figured Twitch was just a sissy.

"Anyway, what happened?" Cody asked.

Twitch decided to briefly explain the highlights as they all listened.

"George picked a fight he couldn't back up. Then all the people at the party jumped into the fight. Some guy was beating on George and another guy ran up to start beating on George, and that's when I punched them off George. George broke free and ran. If we didn't run with him, he would have left us behind. He didn't care about us. We were lucky we didn't get killed."

Cody, Kelley, and George were listening with big smiles on their faces. George had no shame he was the first to run after starting the fight.

Cody was a big guy and had many fights, and Twitch did not, and decided to make a remark, to everyone, not just Twitch.

"That fight gave Twitch a few stripes," Cody joked and laughed with the others.

Twitch assumed the term "stripes" meant rank among his friends and stayed silent. He did not care what Cody or anybody else said about him. He was not going anywhere with George accompanying them. George had a habit of putting his friends in danger. His friends protected him, but George would not protect them.

Pound for pound Twitch was as tough as any of them but not stupid. He was going to fight for George and get himself killed? How stupid could he be? George would not die for him, and he knew it by George's big talk and tall tales and drugged-up mind. Not only was George out for himself and cared less if his friends lived or died, but George's mind had warped into a moron.

In Twitch's eyes George was just a big mouth punk who could not backup the trouble he always started. George was unquestionably the stupidest of them all.

"Okay, Twitch. You sure you're not coming with us?"

"I'm sure," Twitch said adamantly.

"Twitch," Cody said in finality, but with more intensity. "Do *me* a favor and come with us to The Boss Mansion."

"That place is far from a mansion. It looks like a dump," Twitch said. "The last time I was there it was depressing. Full of lowlifes and bums and niggas. I got depressed and left."

"Okay, Twitch. I understand."

Cody hung the phone up and Twitch was happy he made himself clear to Cody and George and Kelley.

After driving around for a while, contemplating if they should go, Cody decided to head for the party in North Miami at George's incessant goading.

George was ecstatic. He knew that petite black tramp was there waiting. He was obsessed with being the first, and not the second to plug her, but would take seconds, or thirds or tenths like any other animal if he had to. It would hurt his pride, but having to wait his turn was better than nothing.

George was licking his chops just thinking of that black filthy tramp. The dirtier she was, the more he seemed to like her.

Cody pulled up at the party, parking his car out front beside the other cars that all seemed jammed together.

Cody put his hand under his seat, pulling out a 9mm and looked at Kelley and said, "Should I take it?"

"No, leave it here," Kelley said. "We don't need it."

Listening to Kelley, Cody would learn, was a grave mistake.

George jumped out, the full force of the drugs twisting his mind. He was a tough guy, bad, and he knew it. And he was the world's greatest lover, and he knew it and would pump that little bitch like she's never been pumped before, and she would never go with another nigga ever again. She would be addicted to him, a Mexican.

Cody and Kelley followed George. Upon entering The Boss Mansion Cody was a little disappointed. Twitch was right. The place looked more like a ramshackle than a mansion. There were about fifty people inside and they looked ragged and worn, full of derelicts, drug addicts, niggas. And the niggas looked like rejects, beggars and ghetto dwellers.

It was depressing. *Twitch couldn't be more right,* Cody thought again. *This place is a dump, a shithole.*

Kelley was used to it and took a seat in the background. He came to sell and nothing else mattered to him. Cody decided to sit with Kelley. Kelley handed Cody a tiny white rock.

"What is it?" Cody asked.

"A half a C-class. It's a strong amphetamine."

Cody popped it into his mouth. He had already taken a Xanax bar and been drinking.

"It won't take more than a couple minutes before you feel it," Kelley assured Cody.

"Thanks," Cody said.

No sooner had they settled in, when there was a loud shouting and Cody and Kelley made out the words. "Come on! Come on!"

Cody and Kelley looked toward the commotion and seen it was George screaming at a group of young black males, challenging them to a fight. At first, the blacks were just ignoring George, acting as if he was not even there.

As the drug took effect, Cody walked up to George, wanting to know what was happening while Kelley stayed in the background monitoring the situation.

"They hit my girl," Gorge yelled, pointing at the little black slut he wanted sex with. "They hit her."

"What business is it of yours if someone hit her?"

"She's with me," George shouted. "I don't like that they hit her."

"George," Cody told him in a rational tone. "She's with anybody who wants to go with her. She takes all of them on. And how can she be with you if you just arrived. She's been here for hours. There's a bunch of niggas already here before you."

In George's drugged-up mind, he was unable to rationalize with Cody.

He was not through yet, becoming more enraged. "And look, look, that dude has his foot up on the chair, blocking my way."

"Just walk around him," Cody said.

George ignored Cody and continued his senseless ranting and mouthing.

Still the Blacks seemed to mind their own business and paid no attention to George. So, Cody walked back to where Kelley was, unsure if George was yelling because they hit his so-called girlfriend or had sex with her first or angry the black dude would not move his foot blocking his way. Either way, he knew George was trying to impress him and Kelley. They knew Twitch was right that George was just a punk, and a wannabe fighter, and hoped he would give up his big mouth arguing.

Everything was quiet for a while, then a few minutes later they heard George yelling again. Then he started yelling more aggressively at the black guy who still did not move his foot. The black guy held his ground, telling George to fuck off. They started arguing louder. The black guy deliberately kept his foot in the same spot. George tried to force his way through. A big scene started developing.

A crowd of blacks started gathering, disgusted with George's big mouth.

George was the type of guy who had a big mouth and a low mind, feeble fighting ability, and wanted to prove to himself and others he was a tough guy.

"Come on, nigga," George screamed. "Come on, nigga."

Through his loud talk, George was hoping to build enough courage to fight.

George was trying to impress Cody too. He felt he impressed Kelley with the last fight he started that could have gotten somebody killed. But George's drugged-up mind could not recognize danger lurking right before him.

The amphetamine Cody took was now taking full effect.

Kelley and Cody were still watching, wondering what was next with this punk George.

George screamed again. "Come on! Come on!"

The black guy had enough of George's mouth and finally sprang to his feet and started rushing George and George hit him. A fight ensued, mostly grappling and pushing and screaming. He was much stronger and pinned George against the wall. George was in trouble, so Cody ran up, jumped into the fight, and hit the black guy once in the face, trying to get him off George. Then some other black guy ran up and hit Cody once in the face and started retreating. It bounced off Cody's face with no effect.

Allegedly Kelley was rushing up now, hoping to break up the fight. When Kelley got next to Cody, shockingly a volley of shots rang out in rapid succession. That was when everybody scattered, the women screaming and running for their lives, the men hiding behind anything they could find. Kelly and Cody instinctively ran behind the stage.

Cody then realized George was not with them. He yelled to Kelley, "George might have gotten shot." Without another word Cody ran back to get George, but George was gone, nowhere to be found.

It turned out the moment the shooting started George was the first to run. Then when he got outside, he suspiciously threw his phone away as if he had something to do with the shooting.

Slowly Cody came walking back to Kelley and Kelley was walking toward him. Kelley was confused why Cody was walking instead of rushing.

The next thing he knew, Cody's voice had changed. It was a weak voice, "I got shot. I got shot. I got shot."

Kelley looked him over and saw no blood then said deeply, "You didn't get shot, man. You didn't get shot."

A second later, to Kelley's horror-stricken eyes, he saw blood pouring out of Cody's chest and back. As Cody was slowly slumping to the floor he kept repeating, as his voice got weaker to almost a whisper, "Kelley, Kelley. I got shot. I got shot, Kelley. I got shot, Kelley." He kept saying it slower, weaker, until his voice faded altogether, and he lay on the floor, moving strangely.

Although someone called the police, the police happened to be close by and rushed in to find Cody covered in blood, lying on the floor, bleeding to death.

According to Kelley, they ordered everybody away from the dying Cody.

George and Kelley stood in the background, instead of rushing up to the police and telling them everything they knew to help apprehend the killer who could possibly still be on the premises. Even as Cody lay on the floor profusely bleeding and dying, they still did not approach the police, just stared in disbelief with the rest of the crowd. They were thinking more of themselves than the dying Cody who put his life on the line for his friends, yet his friends, would never put their lives on the line for Cody. Cody had the right intention to be loyal to the end, but had the wrong friends, friends who were devoutly self-centered, and obviously cared nothing about him. What a tragedy and a disgrace.

About fifteen minutes later the rescue squad and paramedics arrived. They immediately went to work on Cody, realizing he was mortally injured, got him on a stretcher, carried him outside, and by helicopter rushed him to Jackson Memorial Hospital.

Kelley and George continued watching the whole scene unfolding and still never said a word to the police. Many of the people who ran when the shooting started, returned to witness the sad sight of an innocent young man bleeding to death on the floor, with the exception of the Blacks who were rejoicing. It was learned later, the Blacks who came back were actually collecting information on the shooting to bring to the shooter.

Cody got suckered into a fight he never belonged to. It was beyond a shame.

Eyewitnesses said Cody was covered in blood and looked dead as they carried him out and Kelley and George still watched like fools and said nothing.

Any civilized human being would have been appalled at Kelley's and George's behavior.

After the helicopter thudded its way upward then vanished into the night, Kelley allegedly said to George, “Let’s go to the hospital to see if Cody is okay.”

“I can’t,” George said. “I got to go to work in the morning.”

Then George changed the subject with a big smile on his face.

“You see me hit that nigga with everything I had,” George said proudly, still determined to get the attention that he was a tough guy.

“Who cares how hard you hit that nigga,” Kelley said. “Cody’s been shot. Let’s go see him. We got to be sure he’s okay.”

“I got to go to work in the morning,” George repeated resolutely, still proud of starting a fight that got Cody shot.

Cody, bleeding, dying, unconscious, still meant nothing to George. Cody believed he had to be loyal to his friends, blinded to the fact they were not loyal to him. It proved George and Kelley were not Cody’s friends. Friends did not let friends die. Especially when you set them up to die. Even if it was an unintentional setup. At that moment neither man showed remorse for Cody.

Kelley later told Twitch's father he had no transportation so he could not go to the hospital to check up on Cody. Also, he did not want to go alone.

Kelley and George caught an Uber home.

In the morning, Kelley claimed he called Jackson Memorial Hospital and got a connection and was transferred to the operator and he quickly spoke.

"A guy named Cody, 22-years-old got shot, and I want to know if he is okay. Is he doing good?"

"We can't give information like that over the phone. Are you family."

"No, mam, I'm not, just a close friend."

"We only release information to family, sorry."

They both hung up.

By this time Kelly was unsure of Cody's condition but was hoping Cody was okay. Later in the morning he heard the news bulletin that a gunman opened fire at a party and four were shot and one dead. Kelley kept thinking it was not Cody that died because he did not want to believe it.

And George kept telling him, Cody got shot the least serious and the guy who got shot the most serious was the one he was fighting with and was probably the one who was dead. The news bulletin also stated one person was shot by his own people.

By this time Kelley was still hoping that even though Cody was shot up, he was okay.

Kelley immediately called Twitch and his father and said that Cody got shot but was probably okay. Twitch's father immediately called Jackson Memorial Hospital. After about five minutes of being transferred from one recording to another, he hung up.

Listening to the news from Kelley, Twitch thought very little of it until his father turned on the news and he heard, *'there was a young black man shooting in a crowd at The Boss Mansion with one dead.'*

Twitch called Kelley back and said that news bulletin stated that one person was dead. Could it be Cody?

"I don't think it was Cody," he told Twitch. "George said he doesn't think it was Cody either."

"Okay, I'll check up on it, but George's word means nothing to me, because he's only trying to protect himself," Twitch said.

Twitch immediately called friends and told them the news. Most of them thought little of it since they could not fathom that Cody was dead. Cody was too street-smart to get himself killed. But to be sure Twitch called Jackson Memorial Hospital on the spot.

Just like everybody else, he was put on hold for such a long time he could do nothing but hang up, still not thinking the one dead was Cody. And not wanting to believe it.

Cody could not be dead. Again, he and his father both reasoned Cody was too street-smart to die like that.

They both were right but unaware Cody got suckered into that lethal position. Cody would never put himself in a position like that.

Twitch called Kelley back, "I couldn't get through. They had me on hold so long I had to hang up." The thought Cody could be dead horrified Twitch, so he tried his best to deceive himself at the moment. "I agree. I don't think it was Cody," Twitch said. "He's too street-smart." Twitch felt the same way Kelley did, not only because he was in shock and slipping into a state of denial, but Cody taught him how to survive on the streets. How could his mentor be dead?

"Exactly what I was thinking all along," Kelley countered. "I'll call you back."

"Okay."

After talking with Kelley, Twitch and his father felt Cody was fine. Had they been at The Boss Mansion and seen Cody lying on the floor dying they would have known better. But Kelley and George were there, and unknowingly to them Kelley was not offering exact and specific information to them, so how could they know if Cody was dead or alive.

At this moment neither had any reason to think Kelley was lying to them.

Assuming Cody was fine, Twitch decided to go back to work at Miami Subs.

A few minutes after arriving at work, Kelley called Twitch and was crying and saying, "My dawg, my dawg, he's dead."

Twitch was shocked. Could not believe it. Kelley again explained what happened and Twitch finally realized the brightest street-smart guy in the world could fall into a trap and get killed. And George had no doubt set a trap for Cody, regardless intentional or unintentional, Cody was still dead, and George was the blame.

As Kelley was crying Twitch seemed to sense Kelley's crying was a little pretentious.

After Kelley hung up, holding back tears, Twitch told his boss what happened and left the job. When he got home, his father was there, silent and sad.

Twitch screamed and angrily stomped his feet repeatedly around the apartment, his temper rising more every time he screamed and stomped. Twitch continued for about twenty minutes, every second wishing he could get his hands on the killer. And his hate for George escalated.

Twitch lost his best and only intelligent friend.

Then to be certain of Cody's death, Twitch's father turned on the news and there was a repeat of last night's events at The Boss Mansion. Grim-faced, Twitch and his father were riveted to the TV, in shock and desperate to learn the details, hoping and praying Cody was alive and well, although they knew otherwise.

"This is WPLG Local 10 \ Miami News, HELP US CATCH A MURDERER!

"Hello, I'm Detective Edhy Mederos Homicide Bureau, Miami-Dade Police Department.

"On Sunday, April seventeenth, at approximately 9:48 p.m., officers from the intercoastal district were dispatched to the area 151 Street South River Drive in reference to several individuals who have been shot.

"When the units arrived, they discovered multiple individuals suffering from gunshot wounds. Two victims were transported to a local area hospital and unfortunately one of them who was later identified as Cody Clayville succumbed to his injuries.

"Throughout the investigation we were able to determine that several individuals were attending a house party when a fight broke out. During the altercation someone produced a firearm and began shooting recklessly into the crowd causing several individuals to run for their lives.

"Whoever did the shooting had no regard for human life and more innocent people could have died. As a matter of fact, a mother that was picking up her son was struck by bullet fragments and her son who was only fourteen-years-old was also shot in the thigh.

"I have been in constant contact with Cody's parents who still cannot believe that their only child is gone. He was twenty-two-years-old, and he had a long life ahead of him.

"If anyone has information regarding this incident, please call the homicide bureau at 305-471-2400, or you can call Crime Stoppers at 305-471-tips.

"Remember you can remain anonymous and be eligible for a cash reward."

Both Twitch and his father fell into severe mourning. Something had to be done to control those Blacks from murdering Whites. Twitch had AR-15 and AK-47 assault rifles and immediately wanted to go down to the next party and open fire on all the black males. His father felt it was a not a bad idea and was willing to go with Twitch and kill all the black males, but he knew it was just sudden anger and a sudden urge for revenge to rush into. But he convinced Twitch to wait and see if the police picked up the nigga who killed Cody. And by the way, it was George and Kelley's duty to go down there and do the killing anyways.

Twitch gradually agreed with his father. He could not let George implicitly sucker them into being murdered too or killing all the niggas and going to prison for life. George would be boasting to the world he survived a deadly war with the Blacks and did nothing but hide in his house.

Another issue his father contemplated, was that if they did shoot all the black males and got away with their lives, it would only be temporary, because the police would come looking for them and if they did not surrender the police would kill them. He would lose his only child, just like Cody's mother lost her only child. He was not worried about dying at seventy, but could not envision burying his son for something they never were involved in. And in the end, it would have proved senseless, because if they killed a dozen of those Blacks, what if every one of them were innocent and the shooter was still at large? They would be just as bad and stupid as Cody's killer.

Twitch knew his life had fallen apart overnight.

As they were driving, Twitch then called Cody's mother with his father and Kelley at his side.

"Who is this," Cody's mother asked, crying her eyes out.

"I'm James, Cody's friend. I met you before."

He refused to ask if Cody was dead because he did not want to believe it, nor did he want to hurt Cody's mother further.

"Who?" She asked in a scream.

"I'm James. They call me Twitch."

"Oh, I remember you, Twitch." She slowed her crying and screamed. *"Cody's no longer with us."* She cried and cried again. "Cody's no longer with us. He was shot four times in the chest. Cody is no longer with us."

"I know," Twitch said, tears in his eyes. "I'm sorry for you."

"My life is over," she screamed. "My life is over."

Twitch just listened, stayed silent, forcing back tears.

"Thanks for calling, Twitch."

She hung up. She could not bear the grief. The emotional pain was excruciating. Could she survive the disaster?

A few minutes later, Twitch and his father started encouraging Kelley to call Cody's mom. Kelley was silent, appeared pale and hesitant. They felt he was afraid to speak to her.

Guilt could be getting the best of him, they assumed. *Or maybe he was complicit in Cody's death!*

As Kelley sat in the back seat, Twitch in the front, and his father driving, but listening to every word, Kelley put on his speakerphone, and finally called Cody's mother and she instantly broke down, crying and screaming in rage, "Kelly, what happened? What happened to my son?"

"Your son would have been all right, but George started a fight over nothing."

"Do you know who shot my son? Do you know who shot my son?" Her screaming was getting louder and more hysterical.

"There was a whole crowd, a lot of commotion and I couldn't see who was doing the shooting."

She kept screaming and crying and rightfully accusing Kelley of being liable for her son's death. Her sadness and madness had her in a rage.

"Kelly, Cody trusted you. He spoke good about you all the time. He trusted you. Why did you leave my son?" Instinct told her he left Cody.

"*No, mama,* I didn't' leave him." Kelley was in double shock.

"Why did you let my son die, Kelley?"

"*No, mama.* I didn't let your son die."

"You did! You did! Admit it, Kelley!"

"*No, mama,* you're wrong."

"My son trusted you and you let him die," she screamed, directly blaming Kelley.

"*No, mama.* I didn't let him die. It was George."

"You were the oldest and George the youngest. Why didn't you control George?"

"*No, mama. No, mama.* I couldn't control George. He controlled me."

She just kept screaming and crying and accusing Kelley of letting her son die and blaming Kelley for Cody's death. And Kelley kept saying, '*no, mama, no, mama.*' But he knew he was at fault.

Cody's mother was extremely hysterical now and getting worse, still blaming Kelley for Cody's death and had a valid reason for it. Any other parent might want to kill Kelley and George, and the killer as well as kill herself.

Kelley told her the story several times in detail to make her understand. He was obsessed with taking the blame off himself and leveling it all on George.

She could sense Kelley was telling her the truth but leaving out many crucial facts so as not to implicate himself.

She was so inconsolable that Kelley was falling more into shock, a fear he may get the blame for Cody's death and go to prison. He still claimed it was all George's fault.

She kept screaming, "Do you know who did it?"

"*No, mama,* I don't. I was away from the crowd. There was too much commotion and noise and distractions. I was wanting to break up everything, but it all happened too soon. I would have gotten shot too if I had come a second sooner before the shooting started."

She could not stop screaming and crying hysterically. The more distraught she became the more shock Kelly was falling into.

Kelley wished he could cry to alleviate the shock and shame and guilt, but Twitch and his father was beside him, hearing every word Cody's mother was saying.

"What happened to my son?" She screamed and cried and kept repeating. "You were there. He trusted you."

"*No, mama! No, mama.* I don't know what happened."

Kelly kept repeating himself. Telling her the same story over and over.

"Kelly, I don't want to hear that. You were there."

"I did what I can."

Finally, Kelly was almost crying as he spoke.

When he heard the mother crying louder and louder, he felt he would start crying altogether.

"You were like a big brother and was supposed to look after Cody. *He trusted you. He trusted you.*"

"But it got out of hand, out of my control." Kelley defended himself. "At the beginning I was going to break it up and pull George apart from the other guy, but Cody hit the guy and another guy hit Cody as I was about to jump in. Then the shooting happened so fast I didn't get the chance to do nothing.

"George knew who he was messing with. It was all his fault. We were in their territory. We were in Miami. Everybody has guns in Miami. Even kids got guns, thirteen-year-olds."

"You let my son die, Kelly," she continued accusing and still had every right to do so. She knew he was guilty, and he knew he was guilty, though not totally.

Cody's girlfriend was with Cody's mother and had to intervene. She had to help Cody's mother. She was too distressed, and her screaming and crying and mourning was going to kill her.

She had to defend Kelly too. She took the phone from Cody's mother.

"Kelly, she's in mourning. That's why she's talking that way. Don't take it personally."

"Okay," Kelley said and felt better.

Cody's mother got back on the phone, her mourning slightly abating.

"Kelly, what happened? How did my son die?"

Finally, after hearing the story multiple times, and Kelley still blaming it all on George, it started to sway her thoughts and now, she screamed, "*George got my son killed!*"

"*Yes, mama! George got your son killed!* He sure did."

Kelley felt better, relieved she had finally agreed with him, and deliberately blamed it all on George a couple more times, to take the heat off himself, and to be sure she would not change her mind later, he kept repeating the blame on George.

"*Yes, mama. Yes, mama. George got your son killed! Yes he did!*"

He was unable to accept that he was at fault, almost as much as George.

Kelly gave her George's number as a way to sic her on George and to leave him alone.

George claimed he spoke with her and Cody's girlfriend. But Kelley had no proof. Cody's mother and girlfriend did not call Kelley to verify it. He could not believe anything George said. Taking the word of a drug addict was the same as taking the word of a fool.

Twitch had informed Kelley and his father, George was a habitual liar, mentally slow and known to be stupid, a lot more stupid than the average person, a borderline retard, who could get anybody killed. So, if you wanted to live stay away from George.

After all this, he knew George was worried, but not worried a friend of his had died, but worried he may be charged with a crime and go to jail as an accomplice to Cody's murder.

Every time Twitch realized Cody was dead, it hit like a shock, like something impossible, almost like he was extremely scared to believe it, as if he could not believe it. It would give him a fainting feeling, make him gasp for air. He had no choice but to be ready to deal with it, but he seemed to be in a haze.

Twitch reasoned this never had to happen, should have never happened. Yet it did happen. George had to cause trouble to inflate his ego and impress upon his friends he was a tough guy, who could whip anybody, just as long as his friends finished the fight for him.

Labeling George a coward was a compliment. He was a coward's coward. And to complicate matters it appeared he did not care Cody's was dead.

Cody was baffled. What happened? Where was he? Was he alive? He felt very much alive. He dispelled a slight fear rippling through him. Finally, he looked down and saw himself lying on the mansion floor soaked in blood. A lot of people were watching at a distance while the police stood over him.

Then it all dawned on him. He was physically dead, clinging to the last vestiges of hope to live, as he was ascending into the afterlife.

The Blacks had killed him, shot him multiple times in the back since he was white. How much more cowardly can you get by shooting a man in the back?

Where was George and Kelley who claimed they had his back? Then he seen George returning after he ran away when the shots were fired. George started the fight that got him killed and was the first to run when he was shot. And there was Kelley standing on the sideline, doing nothing, watching with the crowd as he lay dying. Kelley did not try to help him. Why? What had he done to Kelley? He did not deserve to be treated like that.

Cody had it now. He recollected everything. When he lay dying, with his last breath of consciousness he thought of his friends. They had run off and left him to die alone! They were not only a total disgrace to their allegedly good friend, but George and Kelley had disgraced themselves.

Was George and Kelley true friends, fake friends, or cowards?

He could have easily answered that himself but even in death he did not want to malign his alleged friends. It did not matter now anyways. George and Kelley would have to live with that for the rest of their lives.

He thought of Twitch asking him what he was doing hanging with Kelley and what was Kelley doing hanging with George since George was below Kelley and Kelly below him. Twitch explained to him multiple time, George was a known troublemaker, but Cody ignored Twitch. Cody realized now that Twitch had given him a direct warning, was trying to warn him to stay away from those guys before something disastrous happened, but he pushed it aside. At this moment, Cody had no regret for ignoring Twitch's warning because it did not matter now.

Even though George and Kelley were on the level of ghetto mentalities, and only thought of saving themselves, they should have at least stayed by his side.

Cody knew they had betrayed him, yet he would have never betrayed them.

As Cody ascended further into the afterlife, he looked down again and saw his mother, girlfriend and stepfather standing over his dead body in the hospital. What touched his heart the most was seeing his mother wailing hysterically. He was truly sorry for putting his mother through this agony, but he never believed George and Kelley would get him killed.

His mother was grieving so severely it was pitiful. Cody never planned on dying at The Boss Mansion, nor putting his mother through this horrible grief.

As he lay dying, he remembered, he was more in shock from the realization he was going to destroy his mother, than from the shock the Blacks had singled him out and shot him down for being white. The Blacks had inflicted cruel death upon him with no just cause or reason, only for being *white.*

But that was racist Blacks for you, though he knew not all Blacks were racist.

He was in disbelief he had suddenly and strangely ended up in a grave for being with the wrong friends, at the wrong place, at the wrong time.

Even in death such extreme sadness gripped Cody to the breaking point. Tears were pouring down his face as he watched his mother grieving. If he could return for just a minute, he would tell his mother he was sorry for causing her such grief. He would tell his mother he would never deal with George and Kelley again. He would tell his mother he would never let her down again. He would tell his mother how wrong he was for destroying her life. And he wished he could tell his mother he knew Kelley and George abandoned him just to save themselves.

How disappointed he was in his friends but far from surprised. He knew George and Kelley would have never died for him the way he died for them, and had no loyalty to him as he had for them, and he knew their friendship was a one-sided, phony deal. Even though George and Kelley's abandoning him was a total disgrace, still he would never malign them.

Cody tried to stem his flow of tears, but it was futile. His tears would never stop, and they poured down his face mercilessly. And he knew why he was weeping, not only for inflicting this horrible grief upon his mother, but because he was terrified his mother may kill herself. He did not want his mother to die. He wanted her to live on and be happy for the remainder of her days.

He understood the agony of his mother losing her only child, pushing her toward suicide. How much could his mother endure. The death of her son was tormenting her beyond belief, past the breaking point. Sadness gripped him still more as he realized suicide for his mother was the only solution that would instantly relieve her grief. He prayed his mother would live on. He loved his mother too dearly to see her die.

Then his mind flashed to the other day, Easter, and he had taken her out to eat. How happy she was, and today, how sad she was. It was all his fault, putting his mother through this tragedy.

He was gone. He hoped his mother would survive. Although his mother may be in mourning for many years to come, she would never forget him. She may never get over his death, but in a few months, she may learn how to deal with it and live on.

Suddenly, all of Cody's grief vanished. The tears stopped flowing. Strangely, he was exalting, confused. Something was happening to him. He could sense he was soaring away, but to where?

Then he saw this huge city with big buildings, blazing with colorful lights and was descending into it. Before his feet touched the streets and walks paved in gold, he saw shops, homes and towers of all shapes and sizes glistening in reds, yellows, pinks, oranges, and colors he never saw before, stretching away into the vastness of happiness. The brilliant colors sparkled and twinkled and shimmered in a mesmerizing display of brilliance and before he realized it, he was laughing.

He was entering the afterlife, and all his tears ceased. He no longer worried if his mother would live on; he knew she would.

Then his feet touched down on a walkway, swirling with liquid silver, gold and platinum. He thought he would sink but he noticed multitudes of people were safely walking on it.

He continued laughing. There was no darkness here. Daylight and colorful lights reigned for eternity.

He was at peace at last.

The day of Cody's death, Twitch and his father both mourned relentlessly, yet neither George nor Kelley made any attempt to avenge his death. Twitch and his father wanted revenge but felt George and Kelley should take care of it. They even believed Kelley and George knew who did it. Even Twitch's father wanted to confront the coward who killed Cody. A shot in the back was the *trademark* of all cowards.

Twitch's father told Kelley to call Cody's mother again to see if they could go and see Cody now, before he was prepared for burial, because he would be more lifelike, but his mother told him they could not see him now. Cody's mother went on to tell him the funeral was planned for the thirtieth of May 2022, almost two weeks after Cody's death and maybe they would not be able to see him at the funeral because Cody's father wanted to keep it a family matter.

But Twitch and his father knew that this *"family matter,"* was just a ruse to keep Cody's so-called friends away because the family knew they were the ones who caused Cody's death. Other than Twitch and his father they were not Cody's friends.

Twitch's father was dismayed and told him to tell her that was not right. They all knew Cody, were friends with him, and wanted to see him, especially now. She finally agreed she would tell Cody's father his friends wanted to see him and to invite them to the funeral. They were all pleased, even if Cody's father still refused.

From morning to night, the next couple days, Twitch, his father and Kelley discussed Cody every single day, hour and minute. They talked about how they would love to find Cody's killer and take the law into their own hands and lynch him, how they would love to go to where the party would be next week and shoot all the black males who were involved in Cody's death, even though they did not know who the black killers were, and how innocent Cody was, and George should have been killed for starting the fight. They shot and killed the wrong person. George was the right person.

Even the homicide detective investigating Cody's murder said that George was the intended target, but Cody ran up just as they were planning to kill George and took the volley of bullets. Cody just happened to run up to the wrong place at the wrong time. It was a shame beyond shame. Or it was an act of fate, that Cody was meant to die that night.

They all kept reliving the sad death of Cody, and each time the reality of how George suckered Cody into his death became more vivid, they became sadder, angrier. What a tragedy that could have been avoided if George could have kept his big Mexican mouth shut. Cody was lying in a casket and George was on Instagram videotaping himself with a joint in his hand and a big smile on his face, showing off his stupidness as usual.

Like all cowards, George refused to take the blame for Cody's death and found a more cowardly way to justify himself and vindicate his actions. He claimed Cody got himself killed, and he had nothing to do with it. He never asked Cody to join in on the fight and get shot to death by a black savage.

Twitch and his father both pointed their fingers at Kelley as an accessory to Cody's death and Kelley continued every tactic to put all the blame on George and clear himself of any wrongdoing. Everybody knew Kelley was not fully the blame, but he should have been in control since he was a full-grown man and should have been able to control the moronic George.

Twitch's father had enough of Kelley's denial of guilt and repeatedly told Kelley that if George was charged with an accessory to murder, there was no doubt in his mind that George was going to implicate him by claiming he was just as much at fault and as guilty as him with the hope of getting off or at least having Kelley in prison with him. George needed Kelley, not only for company but protection, to protect him from the muscle-bound black males who could detect he was a sissy-ass bitch and would rape him silly. They would get him in the showers. And do the job without mercy.

Twitch's father was relentless, and each time he told Kelley, he deliberately explained it in more detail and with more force so it would have more of an impact on Kelley. And each time Kelley heard it he shook his head in fear and disgust and anger and mumbled a profanity under his breath. George had better not drag him into Cody's murder. He still believed he had nothing to do with it.

Twitch, and his father both believed Kelley knew who the killer was but feared he would be targeted by the Blacks if he talked.

Kelley's phone rang suddenly. It was Cody's girlfriend. Twitch and his father were not sure what they were talking about but assumed it was revolving around Cody's funeral.

Kelley was whispering now, confusing Twitch and his father. Why was Kelley whispering? Was there something he was hiding?

Then strangely, to Twitch's father's disbelief, he heard Kelley say, "Where's the piece?" There was a pause then he again said, "The piece. Where's the piece?" Piece meant gun and he was referring to Cody's gun. Apparently, he wanted Cody's gun. Cody had only been pronounced dead hours earlier. What the hell was going on? If Twitch's father could weep, he would weep now.

Twitch and his father were shocked, horrified of the audacity Kelley was displaying. Twitch's father was wishing he had misunderstood the conversation, but he realized he fully understood and was not hearing things. Kelley was allegedly a devoted friend. They better look a little closer at his friendship.

Kelley was in a dilemma. Despite George's betrayal of Cody, he was George's only friend, and wanted to stay friends with him, but knew if he continued being friends with George, his other friends would disown him.

Kelley was unaware his other friends had already disowned him.

On the second- and third-day after Cody's death, it looked like Kelley's mourning was subsiding, but not Twitch's and his father's. It appeared they were both destined to mourn for the rest of their lives.

As Twitch's father mourned relentlessly his anger toward George was mounting by the minute. Why had George lured Cody to his death? George still showed no remorse, just defiance, which proved that anybody he suckered into fighting and dying for him he would treat them the same way he had treated Cody.

Even the day after Cody's death George refused to tell anybody, especially his parents, and each time Kelly, Twitch or his father advised him to call the police and offer any assistance he could to apprehend Cody's killer he became more defiant, claiming he would never tell the *fucking* police anything. Not only was he unable to take his blame, but still feared he could be charged as an accessory to murder. And he was correct. He could be now, tomorrow or years later. There was no statute of limitations on murder.

George was drowning his emotions in drugs. And cared about nothing but himself. He still convinced himself he was a bad street dude, more dangerous than all other street dudes, and Cody's death just added more prestige to his imagined reputation. His mind was warping more by the moment.

Incredulously, George knew no limits to his defiance, and with each passing moment he became more defiant. He incessantly stated it was not his fault Cody was killed. George was so drugged-up it was sickening and pitiful, so everybody gave up on him. He was just a hopeless drug addict.

The thirtieth of May arrived too soon for Twitch, his father and Kelley. The funeral was today.

They had not heard from Cody's mother but assumed Cody's father had agreed to let Cody's friends attend the funeral and they were grateful.

Twitch looked at his father with sadness in his heart and grief on his face and said, "I don't want to see Cody in a casket."

Twitch's father was also in a state of grief and his words could not be more sincere. "I don't blame you, son. I don't want to see Cody in a casket either."

"Every time I think of Cody, I feel worse and scared."

He felt terrible for Twitch. He was Cody's closet friend.

"I understand. I feel horrible and scared too," his father admitted. "What a tragedy."

"Cody lying in a casket keeps flashing through my mind. It's unbearable. I can't repel it no matter how hard I try."

"That's called shock, Twitch. With time you will get over the shock but it's possible you will never get over Cody's death. You'll eventually be all right though. Because you'll learn to live with it."

"I hope so."

"You *will* learn to live with it. I promise you."

Twitch went silent, just listening to his father's conversation, but he worried his state of shock would escalate. He kept envisioning Cody lying in a casket and it was tormenting him. He wanted to see Cody the way he was before his murder. He was wishing for a dream that Cody was somehow alive, but that dream would never come true. Cody was gone and never coming back.

A funeral for a death precipitated by natural causes was one thing, but a funeral of a twenty-two-year-old murder victim was another thing. Cody was robbed of his life. He had a long life ahead of him, but George had unfortunately set him up and a black savage took his life. The Blacks had to be a different species, possibly a species of savages who had no respect for life.

The torment for everybody would not subside. It had been getting worse by the day and now by the minute.

Twitch and his father got into the car and headed for the funeral home. It was a Fort Lauderdale address they never seen before, so they put it in their GPS.

After a half-hour drive, they still could not find it and Twitch called Kelley who was already there. He gave directions to them then hung up.

Twitch looked his father and said with grief, "When I was talking with Kelley, I could hear crying in the background."

"Wow," Twitch's father said emotionally. "That's sad!"

"My God," Twitch said, full of more grief. "What's this world coming to?"

"I wish I knew," his father said. "It's getting worse by the moment."

Silently they drove on. A few minutes later they arrived at the funeral home. Twitch was taking it harder than the rest of them.

They got out of the car and walked inside the lobby. Cody's family was already there. The funeral home was well lit up and did not hold that spooky look of death. No scent of formaldehyde and decaying flesh hung in the air. Twitch was a little relieved as he stood beside his father and Kelley.

They looked around and seen Cody's family members all around them. Two big light-haired young men stood silently, looking at the floor. They noticed both looked a lot like Cody. Although they knew Cody was an only child, it was obvious they were his half-brothers. They were silent, moving about in grief.

Cody's father and stepfather were there, and it showed on their faces if they could get their hands on the killers, they would take the law into their own hands and mete out justice in the same manner their son was murdered. They would butcher those black savages.

They could hear loud crying and grieving in the next room, and as they moved forward, saw it was Cody's mother and Mexican girlfriend. Both were standing over Cody's casket, crying their eyes out. Mourning deeply and angrily, tears pouring down their faces, both dressed in black.

Their mourning was palpable. And scary, but they had to come to grips that this senseless murder was reality.

The sight of Cody in the casket was devastating. Twitch was horrified and he knew his life was forever changed.

The mourning and the sight of Cody's body brought tears to Kelley's and Twitch's and his father's eyes.

Cody was clad in a red suit with a gold chain around his neck, his dark hair neatly combed. He was robbed of his life for no rational reason. And of course, George set it up but would deny it to the end of his life.

Cody looked like he was sleeping and could awaken at any moment. But they knew he would never rise again.

Kelley sat on a bench beside the casket as Twitch and his father moved toward the casket and stood behind Cody's mother and girlfriend who slightly blocked their view, but they stared at Cody's face for a long while in deep sadness and pity.

Twitch and his father saw Cody's face reflected severe pain and anger. The pain that his friends were actually his enemies. The anger that he actually died for them without knowing they were his enemies, and not wanting to believe it. In death now, he certainly not only knew they were his enemies, but believed it. How Cody had duped himself! But that could have happened to anybody out of loneliness, and a false belief, since he was loyal to them, they were loyal to him.

After a while they sat down, but Cody's mother and girlfriend remained leaning over the casket and mourning. Cody's mother was being held up by a man and a woman on both sides of her. Otherwise, she would have collapsed to the floor as the grief was wracking her mind, body, and soul. It was a pitiful sight no parent would ever want to endure.

Cody's mother was in such distress, it looked as if her life was over. Her only child was murdered. Her and Cody's father were in disbelief. They could not believe their only child was gone.

Twitch kept reliving Cody's death, still horrified, certainly aware his life had changed forever and for the worse. He never again wanted to see another black person.

The thought of going to the party and walking in with his AK-47 and shooting all the black males kept flashing through Twitch's mind. It seemed like it would not go away and was goading him into action. The thought was tempting but he knew it would not bring Cody back.

His father was not a violent man but felt violent today and if the killers were there, he would personally slit all their throats. He would love to get his hands on Cody's killers. He also knew shooting them would guarantee a life sentence in prison or even the death penalty or death by resisting arrest.

Revenge was also on the minds of many others. They would love to see how the Blacks would feel seeing their own kind getting shot down like Cody. The innocent Blacks. How would they like it? How would they handle it? How would the black mothers deal with it?

Probably, in the same manner the Whites were taking Cody's death. Vengeance and hatred would be preying on their minds too. But of course, they would victimize themselves and say they were singled out and killed because they were black. And every white fool in the nation would buy the story. What about Whites being murdered by Blacks? You never hear about that.

Well, the ironic issue here Cody was undoubtedly singled out by the Blacks because he was white. But in the minds of the Blacks, it was justified if they killed innocent Whites but unjustified if Whites killed guilty Blacks. The world had gone to hell.

As Cody's mother and girlfriend continued to lean over the casket and mourn and grieve, family members and friends of Cody's girlfriend walked in and joined them near Cody's casket. Several Mexican men walked up and hugged Cody's girlfriend and whispered to her, expressing their condolences and sympathy, hoping to ease her grief. But it did no good, for her mourning continued unabated. A couple Mexican women hugged Cody's girlfriend and cried and stood by her side.

Finally, Cody's mother was held up and led away by Cody's stepfather and put into a chair where her mourning continued.

Anger and grief and vengeance still showed on Kelley's, Twitch's, and his father's faces. They were not crying physically but were crying mentally.

More people arrived at the funeral. Most went up to the casket and stood over Cody, silent, grief-stricken, in disbelief and shock.

Cody's mother was helped back to the casket. Then her grief was vented again, louder, sadder. She cried, and mourned, and cried, and grieved. She still was inconsolable. Her only child was gone. He was robbed of his life. By a bunch of savages. Armed black men shooting unarmed white men. Cowardice had no end.

Cody's girlfriend was still leaning over the casket, her grief and weeping never ceasing.

Twitch's father inched back to the casket. He stared sadly at Cody. Tears were in his eyes. Twitch followed and stood beside him, filled with grief, then Kelley was there, silently mourning. Twitch was the closest to Cody and of all his friends, was taking it extremely harder. Cody's death was going to plague him for the rest of his life.

They all felt sad for Cody's mother. Just looking at her. She would never get over it. She would take her grief to the grave.

Cody's father and stepfather were mourning too but they held it in. They had to be supportive of Cody's mother and girlfriend. They shed no tears, but they shed much grief.

What really angered Twitch's father was that Cody was shot in the back, like his younger brother many years earlier. Cowards. Shooting unarmed people in the back.

More people were arriving at the funeral and most of the chairs were filled.

Willie's father stepped away from the casket, took a tissue and wiped the tears from his eyes then wiped his nose.

A woman walked up to him in the lobby.

"How do you know Cody?"

"From my son. Cody started coming over the house to see my son when he was fifteen."

"Who are you?"

"I'm Cody's stepmother." Twitch's father thought he heard correctly but was not certain due to heavy stress overwhelming him.

"Oh, nice to meet you."

They both looked at each other for a few seconds then Willie's father was compelled to say, "It's all George's fault. He started the whole fight that got Cody killed."

"Shhhh," she said, "this isn't the time to talk about that."

"You're right," Willie's father said. His deep sadness for Cody and harsh anger for the Blacks and George had overwhelmed him.

They had a few more words before they both slowly walked away. Twitch later told him he was talking to Cody's Aunt Shayne.

Could they really blame the Blacks? His father thought. *The Blacks, the majority of them, were savages, the same family of the Whites but of a different species. Maybe even subhuman. They had no value for human life. They had no value for their own lives. Wrong to them was right and right to them was wrong.*

He was not racist, although the few educated Blacks would call him racist to unleash their sick propaganda, but the handwriting was on the wall, and every indication pointed at their savagery and animalism. Only animals killed for no reason and had no regard for human life. The Blacks had to be separated from the Whites or more disaster would fall upon the Whites.

He took a seat again beside Twitch and Kelley, his grief escalating and his anger mounting uncontrollably. Something had to be done with these Blacks.

The mourning and weeping of Cody's mother still had not abated and seemed to be intensifying. She could not walk without help or she would fall to the floor. Her husband held her up as she still lingered over Cody's casket.

About a half-hour later, a minister arrived, a young black man, to preach the sermon. He was clad in jeans, a short sleeve shirt and his muscles hung out and gave him the appearance of a thug.

He stood behind the lectern and spoke as eloquently as he could, calmly, stoically, devoid of emotion.

"We are here today to remember and respect the memory of Cody Clayville whose life was taken many years too soon and without cause."

To Willie's father he sounded more like a street thug than a minister.

The minister quoted verses from the bible for a few minutes, interpreted them, mentioning death was an act of the devil and all evildoers would someday face Judgment Day. The more he preached the more thuglike he appeared, not sounding anything like a minister.

The audience was silent save for the mourning of Cody's mother and girlfriend.

The minister suddenly went silent, looked over the mourners and looked like he was running out of words, so he immediately changed topics.

"I've been to prison four times in my life before I came to God. If it weren't for my prison sentences, I may have never come to God."

That was it for Twitch's father. He had heard more than enough. He had been right all along. Not only had the minister been a thug at a time in his life but had spent time in prison and now was preaching the word of God. Was it a pretense, a way to make easy money? He did not have to steal anymore and face a jail term, had people giving him money and there was no law against that. He felt they would have been better off had they not had a minister there, at least this minister.

So, changing from a thug to a minister was the same as hiding behind the name of God and making a living out of it.

The minister continued and finally made some sense, *"If you really want to please this young man who lies in this casket, you can start by helping the family get through this difficult time."*

The minister looked over at a man standing a few feet from him. *"Thanks for giving me this opportunity to be here."*

"You're welcome," the man said.

The minister gathered his papers and quickly and quietly left the funeral home.

The funeral was over. He wondered how much the minister would get paid for speaking more nonsense than sense.

People began to talk among themselves.

Cody's mother's grief ceased a bit, but she was still mourning. She was led back to a chair. Cody's girlfriend still appeared to be in shock as her mourning slightly abated.

Twitch's father was feeling a bit better but was still in shock. Twitch was feeling the worst. He could not understand how Cody ceased to exist. And he would never see him again.

His father walked back up to the casket and stared at Cody with pity for a few minutes. If anybody ever suffered an injustice, it was Cody. He seemed unable to take his eyes off Cody. He was full of hatred toward the Blacks and George and Kelley.

Kelly suddenly walked up to Twitch's father's left and stood over the casket. It was hard to tell what was on his mind. Then Kelly patted Cody on the chest so hard the casket moved a few inches as he said. "Okay, Cody, man, I'll be seeing you." He walked back to his chair, leaving Twitch's father alone beside the casket.

Then the undertaker stood beside the casket too and took off the gold chain around Cody's neck.

His father looked at him and said, "Can I take a few pictures."

"Sure," he said.

With cell phone in hand, Twitch's father took a total of five pictures at different views. He was taking the pictures so he could always remember Cody till the end of his days, and he knew Twitch and other people would want to see Cody, even if it was in death.

He wanted Cody to never be forgotten.

Although he was not related to the family, he still had this insane urge to go to the next party with his AK-47 and shoot all the black males, one after the other, believing they were all involved, and the shooter was among them. It kept echoing through his mind. *'Do it! Do it!'* But he kept fighting the insane urge. *He could hear the black killers right now saying with pride they shot and killed a cracker,* he thought. *There was one less cracker in the world.*

The thought was angering him to the point of insanity, but he knew he could not do it. Twitch would be fatherless. And would end up dead himself or in a crazy house.

Gradually the mourners began to vacate the funeral home. Cody's girlfriend was scared to go home alone so Kelley and Twitch got in the car with her and drove off against his father's will. His father felt that Kelley and Twitch leaving with her was irreverent to Cody and to his family, especially as the family watched them all leave together.

Cody's girlfriend stated repeatedly she did not ever want to leave the apartment because of all the memories of her and Cody there.

Finally, Twitch's father asked if Cody would be buried in the graveyard outside the funeral home. He was told that Cody was to be cremated. That even added more grief to him, and Twitch. They preferred to have Cody buried so they could visit him every once in a while. But it was the family's decision, and they had no say in the matter.

Twitch's father took a final pitiful look at Cody as they vacated the funeral home. Sadness still gripped their hearts.

Cody was all alone now as he was all alone as he died, and now awaiting the furnace all alone.

Cody would never be forgotten.

If Cody had any consciousness, he would probably shake his head in dismay and in disbelief he was again all alone. What a disaster!

People began to get in their cars and drive off.

Twitch and Kelley were long gone. Twitch's father seen Cody's mother and stepfather and walked up to their car.

"Cody got killed because he was set up," Twitch's father explained.

"What for?" Cody's stepfather asked in disbelief.

"From what I understand it was an unintentional set up," he said. "George started a fight he couldn't handle, and Cody tried to help, and they opened fire on Cody. Even the homicide detective investigating the case says Cody was not the intended victim. It was George."

They stared at Twitch's father in dismay for a minute then slowly drove off, still full of grief and disbelief, their only child was dead.

Twitch's father was one of the last to leave. He did not want to go. This was the last time he would ever see Cody. He drove off full of grief, anger, and hatred.

The race Cody trusted and embraced was the race that killed him. All the white people at the funeral learned they could never turn their back on a black man again. Not all Blacks were alike, but one was enough to put them on guard against the entire race.

After the funeral and upon hearing Kelley talk to Cody's mother, denying everything, and assessing all the details of Cody's death, Twitch's father told Twitch to let Kelly know to stay away. He no longer wanted anything to do with Kelley since Cody went out with him and came back dead.

Kelley used to live with them. Twitch's father considered Kelley like a family member. But not anymore. If he went out with Kelley, he might come back in a casket too. He did not want anything to do with that.

"Okay, Dad, I'll tell Kelley."

"Thanks, son. Please tell him in a polite way."

Twitch's father reasoned that had it been Twitch that got murdered instead of Cody, Kelley and George would have both pumped him full of shit like they pumped Cody's mother full of shit. It was not like they lied to her. They just told her what they wanted her to know, enough facts to know how Cody died, but left out enough facts so they would not have to admit their wrongdoing.

George's and Kelly's manipulation was enraging Twitch's father.

Early that morning, Twitch met up with Kelley and immediately opened up to him.

"Listen, my father doesn't want to be around you anymore because he says he feels haunted. He said you spooked him. He still likes you but wants nothing to do with you anymore. He says it's nothing personal and to let you know that."

"It's because of Cody's death, right?" Kelley asked.

"Of course, it's over Cody's death."

Kelley was good friends with his father and did not want to lose that friendship and became defensive.

"What do you mean? He wasn't there. He didn't see Cody get shot and fall on the ground."

"He didn't want to see Cody get shot and fall on the ground, Kelley! And he told me if he went out with you, he might get shot and come home dead. And he stressed to me multiple times not to go anywhere with you ever again because I might come home dead."

Kelley was trying to defend himself for a while then reasoning set in. He knew he was partially liable for Cody's death.

"I didn't mean to make it sound too bad," Twitch said. "My father told me to break the news to you as politely as possible. He doesn't understand why you didn't help Cody when he was dying on the floor."

Kelley looked sad and guilt settled deep into his soul.

"Yeah, I understand," Kelley said. "I'll stay away."

That night, after Cody's funeral, Twitch, exhausted and terribly stricken by Cody's death, fell into a heavy but disturbing sleep. He tossed and turned most of the night. Then he started dreaming. It was terrifying and tormenting. In his dream he kept trying to wake himself up by jerking his body. After the third time, he woke with a jolt. He was shaking and covered in sweat. The dream was so real, he was not sure if it was a dream. A couple minutes later he was okay.

As soon as his father came to see him, Twitch opened up to him. He had to talk to somebody. The dream was eating at his nerves. They were silent as Twitch spoke.

"I had a dream of Cody: my phone rang, and his phone number showed up on the screen, and I expected Cody's mother to answer, because I knew he was dead. But it was Cody; it was like he was alive. The conversation started and he immediately said, "Twitch, they shot me, cuz.

"Then we started talking back and forth about stuff we usually talk about. Hearing his voice made me feel he was not gone. Like he was here.

"In my mind I knew Cody was dead, but the call felt like it was Cody alive on the phone."

Twitch fell silent. His father was silent, could feel the hurt in Twitch's tone and the horror in his mind. Due to his grief, describing the dream was severely disorganized and distorted.

Twitch started again.

"Then I had another dream, and in the dream, we were with black people and one of the black guys looked like Cody. His face had Cody's face. It had turned from black to white. Then he told people there's Cody and they said it's not. He had morphed into Cody's face and I was thinking it was Cody.

"Someone said there's Cody and others said no it's not. I was looking at Cody with my eyes squinted and jaw half-opened and eventually realized it was something only he wanted to believe, and it wasn't Cody. It was unbelievable to see Cody gone off the earth. Something that felt like a movie. Something too coincidental to what I had feared to be natural causes, like something like divine power in control.

"I woke up trembling and shivering and still in disbelief Cody was gone, shot dead by a savage black guy."

His father stared at Twitch with deep sad thoughts.

"You're still in shock, Twitch," his father said. "Actually, you are in a horrible state of shock. Sure sounds like it."

Twitch stayed silent, feeling as if in a dream, unable to comprehend the senseless murder of Cody, unable to accept Cody was never coming back to the earth.

Twitch's father continued.

"And you are in a horrible state of mourning."

Twitch fell silent, just listened, as his father continued.

"You will have to live your life without Cody," Twitch's father said, hoping Twitch could accept it and move on.

"That bastard will pay for what he did," Twitch said.

"Absolutely. No bad deed goes unpunished," his father said, hoping to mollify Twitch's grief. "The shooter will end up getting murdered himself, if the police don't pick him up first."

Twitch confessed in a whisper. "I feel like I'm trapped in a horror movie. A horror movie with no end or escape."

Twitch was not crying outwardly but it was obvious he was crying inwardly.

His father hoped Twitch would survive this horrible ordeal. It was taking a mental toll on him. He had a close friendship with Cody and seemed unable to go through life without Cody.

The next day Twitch was talking to his father about Cody and said, "As I stood over Cody's casket, I saw stitches on Cody's head. Does that mean they cut his head open?"

"I think so," his father said. "I think it's state law to take out the brain and weigh it."

"I don't want that to happen to me when I die," he said. "I don't want them cutting me up and removing my organs. I heard Cody's father allowed the hospital to remove Cody's corneas."

"Really? I don't like that."

"Neither do I."

"We'll check into a Muslim funeral when the time comes for both of us since we are of Arabic descent. I don't think they embalm you, just put you in a box and bury you."

"They do?"

"Yes, I think so. It's similar to a Jewish funeral. They want you to return to the dust of the earth in the same way you came from it."

Twitch knew he would still be in shock over Cody's death for many years to come, if not for his entire life.

"When they embalm you do you stay like that forever or do you still rot away?"

"It depends how much formaldehyde they pump into you. If they pump a little bit into you, you rot away faster. If they pump a lot into you, you may never rot away."

"You mean if they dug me up years later, I would look the same as I did when they buried me? I wouldn't want that when I die. I want to rot away as quickly as possible."

"I feel the same way, son. I want to rot away quickly too. My reason is not only because of our ethnicity, but I have this fear that maybe I will wake up inside the coffin after they bury me."

"Yeah, that would be scary," Twitch said. "If I go first make sure my entire body is intact and bury me immediately, without embalming me, and I'll do the same for you if you go first."

"Okay, son," his father said.

Shortly after the funeral and many times afterward Twitch would approach his father and say, "First it's like a shock you don't understand, then the sadness comes, then anger comes, then hatred comes, and you unwillingly accept it.

"It still makes you want to go down to Miami and shoot all the black niggas." He was extremely distraught. It seemed the more time that passed the more grief-stricken he was.

"You're exactly correct, son," his father said. "Please, son, do not attack the Blacks without notifying me because I would never let you go down there by yourself and commit a slaughter. I wouldn't want you to kill anybody but if you were, I would go with you because I would rather die with you than to go through what Cody's parents are going through.

"First, you got to understand not all the Blacks there that night when Cody was murdered are involved in it and if you just shot all the black males at random, God only knows how many of them would be innocent victims like Cody. So please let's let the police handle it. If we did commit a slaughter, it would be headlines today and forgotten tomorrow. They would all be dead, and we would be dead. Please listen to your father. I would not want to hear you died down there all alone. I would die of a broken heart, probably like Cody's parent are going to do. I don't believe Cody would want that anyways. Sacrificing your life and taking the lives of multiple black males when only one or several were guilty makes no sense. Don't think it does not anger me as much as it does you.

"It's been a couple months now and there's not a moment in the day that I don't think of Cody and how he was suckered into dying for George. Death or prison would be the end result of committing a slaughter. We both would be better off dead than going to prison for life. If you really want to help Cody and his family let's help the police find the cowards that killed him. Shooting a man in the back is extremely angering. But that's cowards for you. Now let's try to move on with our lives. The police will eventually find the cowards."

"Okay," Twitch agreed.

"If an injustice had ever been committed, it was against Cody."

They talked about Cody every day and almost all daylong for weeks, then the weeks turned into months and still there was not a day they did not speak about Cody for at least a couple hours.

Twitch still openly mourned over the loss of his close friend, along with his father.

One day he came to his father and unleashed his feelings toward his so-called friends.

"After all this time I've had enough of my friends, like Kelley and George. And all these homeless people I met and was doing business with them on the street, they finally had an indelible impact on me, as if they stamped me like a tattoo with all their drugs, abuse, and negativity, as if I'm forever trapped with them. They finally corrupted me, damaged me. When it comes to Kelley, he doesn't matter to me anymore. And George, he never mattered to me.

"It was too big of a deal what those two did to Cody. They can't even comprehend what they lost. Cody was intelligent. They're far from it. Cody just made a bad mistake like many young men his age. They're just a *nothing* all the way around. I had enough of them. How many times I told these guys not to start trouble. They didn't listen and got my closest friend killed. They lost their rank in street society. Not George. He never had any rank, but Kelly did and now he lost it all.

"It would be pretty much the same as if it happened to me. Let me die and claim to my family they did nothing wrong. That it was my fault, and they just happened to be with me, and claim they wanted to help me, but the police would not let them. Yes, it would be no different.

"They punished Cody's mother, put her on the edge of suicide. I'm not dealing with those guys anymore. They don't care. It's a shame. Cody's family knows George and Kelley told them a little truth and a lot of lies and told them only what they wanted them to hear, not everything that happened. And they would have lied to you just as they lied to Cody's mother. They know we know they are evading the important issue, mixing lies with a little truth, but they have no shame.

"How many times have I told you what you just told me?"

"I know. I know. I just can't forget what they did to Cody."

"Nobody can forget what they did to Cody."

His father was still horribly angry at them for letting Cody die. And worse, not even coming to his aid. and trying to help comfort him as he lay dying, not even attempting to assure him he would be okay, not even trying to stem the flow of blood as he lay dying, no attempt to save Cody, nothing, nothing. What a disgrace.

"It's beyond a shame what they did to Cody and his parents," his father said.

"When Cody's mother first learned, her only child was murdered she told me, screaming and weeping, *her life was over.* I didn't know what to say. I didn't know what to do. Her exact words were, *"My life is over.* Screaming out relentlessly and repeatedly *her life was over!* I can't even explain her grief. It was a nightmare for her as well as for me, and to this day I can still hear her screaming.

"What happened to Cody could have easily happened to me. I know those dudes. After being around them, I know how they are. It's a miracle I kept myself alive when hanging around them.

"They took Cody's innocence and led him to his death.

"They let it happen and on top of that look at the way they handled it, lying about it, justifying it, refusing to take the blame. That's the way I look at it. They let it happen."

"I can feel your grief, son, because I'm full of grief too. For now, let it go, son."

His father was thinking on the same terms as Twitch and reiterated. "You know, I have always known that if that had happened to you, they would have lied to me as they did to Cody's mother. But Cody's blood is on their hands and let them deal with it. I sure wouldn't want to be in their shoes."

Without informing his father, Twitch went back to the party a couple weeks later armed with his 9mm. and loaded with a thirty-bullet clip and asked around about Cody's killer. He was ready to use it if he had to. He mentioned many times he was not going to die like Cody: get ambushed, not a chance to fight back. He would die fighting with the 9 mm. If a fight was coming down, he would open it up first, get the drop on them, take many niggas with him. But if they knew he was armed, they would backdown and live to fight another day when they could ambush him when he was unarmed.

He was sad Cody did not have the chance to fight back. He was just ambushed, unknowingly walked right into the line of fire. Had he been a second late, George would have been lying dead on the floor instead of Cody since George was the intended victim. And no doubt, Cody would have run to his side and helped him till the police arrived.

He just hoped if he had to kill it would be the killer he shot. He recognized a girl at the party who was there when Cody was killed and questioned her. She told him she knew who killed Cody and said his name was Jerry then walked away. She came back a few minutes later and said, "I know who killed your homeboy."

Twitch listened as closely as he could, hoping to get as much information as he could.

"And his name is Jerry," she repeated.

Twitch talked to her longer, wanted to know how she knew it was Jerry.

"I used to date him," she said. "He was my boyfriend."

"What's your name and phone number? And do you mind if the detective on the case calls you?"

"It's okay, just keep it quiet. I don't want Jerry to know. And my name is Karen." He watched as she texted her phone number to him.

Twitch thanked her and saw her leaving the party with Camillo, a friend of his."

The next day Camillo told him the girl freaked out as he was driving her home and made him pull over on I-95 and got out. She was freaking him out too, by her strange behavior, and was glad to see her go, as she kept saying the Blacks were going to kill her for telling you Cody's killer's name.

The next morning, Twitch gave the information to *Crime Stoppers* Detective Edhy Maderos, who was on the case. When the detective called her, she was quite cooperative, and told the detective the same story. But the problem arose when she admitted she never actually seen the shooter but heard it was Jerry. And nobody else came forward to substantiate her story so they could not pick Jerry up.

She wanted to get that $5,000 reward *Crime Stoppers of Miami* had put out for the killer's arrest.

Later that day the detective called for Twitch, but his father answered the phone. He asked his father to tell Twitch to get information on this Jerry.

"I won't let my son go there by himself," he told the detective, "So I will have to go with him and if I go, I'm telling you right now, I'm going armed and will cut down any threat to us without any hesitation or worry of consequences."

"No," the detective said. "I would never put you or your son in danger by going there. I mean to go on social media and get information on this Jerry. With the information I can find out who he is."

"Okay," his father promised. "When I mentioned going armed, just wanted to let you know we're not going out like Cody. We'll shoot anybody with the slightest provocation of putting our lives in danger."

"I understand," the detective said, "and I don't blame you."

They hung up.

When he seen Twitch, he told him what the detective said. Twitch did not make the response his father assumed he would.

"How are we going to find Jerry on Facebook or YouTube?" Twitch asked. "If anything, this guy Jerry, if he is Cody's killer is going to keep his mouth shut to save his own life or stay out of prison."

"That makes sense," his father said. "I'm not sure what the detective meant when he said to go on social media."

"You should have asked him," Twitch said.

"I know I should have. But didn't think of it at the time."

"That's okay," Twitch said. "I know criminals are stupid but still I don't think he is stupid enough to go on social media and post what happened at The Boss Mansion."

His father nodded in assent.

For the hundredth time, Twitch and his father both wished they could get their hands on Cody's killer. They would mete out justice the way it should be. Take the law into their own hands. They would be the judge, jury and executioner without seeing the inside of a courtroom.

Night after night Twitch was having recurring nightmares of Cody's death. He confided in his father mostly but also continued to discuss it with Kelley. Kelley just listened, rarely talking, seemingly in a strange state of mind. Twitch knew torment and guilt was still plaguing Kelley from morning to night.

As time passed and Cody's murder remained unsolved, Twitch eventually put Cody in the background as he tried to get back on with his own life, although he never forgot the sad and senseless death of Cody, and would still help solve the murder, if any new information came up.

It was only a matter of time before the law picked up the black killer that killed Cody anyway.

If he did not get away from the memory of Cody, and grief of Cody's murder, he would be mourning for the rest of his life.

He felt almost as sad for Kelley because he sensed Kelley would be mourning for the rest of his life too, especially with disbelief mercilessly eating away at him.

George was another issue. He was probably too overwhelmed with drugs to even remember Cody's murder. A total waste.

Twitch would have invited all his black friends of Liberty City and Brownsville to the funeral, but he feared Cody's family, if they saw all the Blacks there, would go berserk since it was Blacks that killed Cody. At this stage, Twitch reasoned, Cody's family could not distinguish the good Blacks from the bad Blacks. To them all the Blacks were the same. They were slightly wrong, because not all ghetto Blacks were alike, just about ninety percent were.

Willie did not want to hurt Cody's family anymore. They had been hurt enough.

His image of Blacks now was different, changing by the day. He talked about them in an opposite way. Before they were all his friends, and he believed he could trust them. But that was in the past and now he seen them all as a potential threat, a potential enemy, not only to others, but also to himself.

Even though he had many black friends, he reasoned that they may decide to kill him, merely for being white. He had to be on guard, watch their movements, decipher their words, or to just stay away from them altogether.

He told his father his true feelings now, and he was ecstatic and urged Twitch not to delay, just dump them immediately, to associate with his white roots only where he would be safe and where he belonged. But as usual, Twitch was just as stubborn now as he was in the past and agreed to only limit his friendship with the Blacks, to the dismay of his father, even if there could be dire consequences.

"They killed your best friend, boy! Are you forgetting that? What's wrong with you? You want to end up dead too?" Then he attacked Twitch head-on with full force. "I'm sure if Cody could rectify his mistake right now, he would. He would never deal with Blacks again."

As sad as he was that the Blacks had killed his best friend, he still did not want to label all of them as killers.

"Dad, are you insinuating all the Blacks in the world are killers?"

"Insinuating! Are you crazy. Just turn on the TV and watch any news station and the first thing you see are the Blacks murdering their own people without being arrested. They are expanding their horizons and spilling white blood just to say they killed a cracker. I told you before it's status for a Black to murder a White. Boy, you are having trouble seeing light from day. Who do you want them to kill next? Someone in your family so you can continue to mourn for the rest of your life?"

Twitch knew his father was insinuating they might kill the most important person in his life: *his father.* And revenge would be the silliest thing in the world. No severity of revenge, no quantity of revenge, would replace his father.

Just to placate his father but to seriously consider it later, he said, "Maybe you're right. Maybe I better analyze my association with the Blacks."

And it did pacify his father. Maybe Twitch was sincerely considering it. And he hoped the first person he would dump was Kelley. Twitch was suffering enough over Cody's death and did not need more suffering to befall him.

Twitch reminisced on his dead friend; Cody gone in just a short time. He never expected it, never had a reason to believe he was going to die that night. Simply because he was doing nothing wrong.

And his father was right. *Who was next,* he thought? Then he amplified the thought in his mind. He was face to face with a realization that it could be him. Maybe sooner than later, the Blacks would turn on him.

It appeared that Blacks lacked courage because their victims were usually unarmed. It was easy for an armed Black to kill an unarmed man. They could kill at will and not worry about dying themselves. They did not mind killing, just did not want to die. And they murdered their own people by the day, by the minute, exemplifying their disregard for human life.

It was sad but true.

And what made the Blacks dangerous, they were lucky if they had a third-grade education. And what made them more dangerous, they were ignorant. Their behavior exemplified it.

Even worse, they were welfare babies, like their parents, grandparents, great-grandparents, who were mainly illiterate and knew no other life than welfare. *Poverty and illiteracy were the two main ingredients to violence.*

So, in a sense you could not fully blame their violence on them, because their culture called for violence, but in another sense, you could blame it on them, because they did not have to follow that way of life. But they followed it, possibly because it was the easiest way of life. Many of them may not know right from wrong, but many of them did know right from wrong. Not every black man was stupid, just the majority of the uneducated Blacks. Now the black-on-black violence had spread to the white community, and Whites were being murdered. With impunity, the Blacks were spilling white blood and gleeful over it.

It had to stop even if the Whites had to take the law into their own hands.

And the torment refused to stop. Even a year after Cody's death, Twitch awoke in a panic late one night. He was so worried his mind could not handle it. He was trembling, terribly shaken, displaying a confused look and confided in his father.

"Dad, I had another dream about Cody, almost identical to all my dream, but this dream was more vivid, more real. And afterwards, other dreams followed."

"Go ahead. Tell me about them. I'm listening."

He was praying his son would not have a mental breakdown. The torment was still preying on his mind as intense as it was a year ago. When would homicide solve Cody's case? It would take pressure off Twitch, maybe even save his sanity.

"In the first dream, I got a call from Cody's phone and when I answered it, again I assumed Cody's mother would be on the other end. But it was Cody again, and he was alive, but what made it strange, is that I knew in my dream that Cody was dead in life, but he seemed so real on the phone and his voice was like he was alive talking to me. It sounded just like him, word for word, even the tone of his voice was the same as in life. I took the phone away from my face and sitting there with a confused look, like he's dead but he's here on the cell phone as if he is not erased from life."

Twitch was full of dread, stuttering, repeating himself pitifully.

"He's gone but on the phone he's here. Again, we talked about a lot of things like we did when he was alive. He said yeah, cuz, them niggas had shot me.

"Then I don't remember the other things we talked about, but it was like a routine conversation, talking about what's new for about five minutes and like what happened. Then I got off the phone a little puzzled and didn't think much of it. We hung up like nothing happened, like all right bro.

"Then strangely he called back almost immediately. And this time we talked about when he died. How he died. Why he died. And why they ain't found them niggas who killed him.

"Then I said to him, *I know you're dead,* but he did not answer me and continued to talk about other things. Cody went on until I was almost paralyzed in fear."

"Wow, that's amazing," his father said.

"I knew he was dead in my dream," Twitch said again, forcefully holding back his weeping. "But he seemed to be alive, like he was real, and it seemed so real, and his voice was the same. Then I woke up."

The dream had a big impact on Twitch because he talked about it for the next couple days.

Shortly after that, Twitch even had another dream about Cody.

"We were driving somewhere as we did when Cody was alive, and Cody was speeding in the car. Just me and Cody riding around in the car around Woodside. Somehow a girl was in the car with us, and he gave her a ride and the girl wanted us to run her around. Cody was being friendly about it. Then the dream faded."

Twitch had a number of dreams of Cody after that and did not know what to think of them. He stopped telling his father of most of the dreams because his father talked a lot about them and asked him a lot of questions he could not answer, and his father knew he was possibly forever tormented by Cody's death.

Twitch did not seem scared now, just grieved, concerned, baffled. Even in his dreams he knew Cody was dead. But Cody was refusing to admit he was dead.

Twitch's father kept hoping Twitch would not have a mental breakdown and end up in a nut house.

The dreams seemed ceaseless, endless, driving Twitch's emotions to the ground.

Then he had another dream, and the fear struck again with such relentless intensity, he was compelled to tell it to his father.

His father listened with a deadpan face. He knew dreams were so jumbled and garbled that at times they made no sense, so he made it a point to listen as closely as possible as Twitch spoke.

"In my dream, I was searching to see who did it to Cody. I got some news, like at the party. Since I came up on some news, I thought I would come up on more news. I met up with a lick, the one I met a long time ago. I heard there was talking that somebody shot and killed somebody. Then a black guy said he shot and killed somebody and was worried. An even though, Cody's name was not mentioned, I knew it was Cody.

"I said, you feel like superman kind of, as a joke. The guy took me in his house, and I saw a picture of Cody in his house. He then said it was a guy named Cody. The guy had slowly realized it was my friend, and I was in the guy's house.

"He had a few guns around and as he was talking, he asked if Cody was my friend and I thought what if he picks up that gun and shoots me, but I know he won't because he was scared.

"So, I tell him all right, I'll see you later because I didn't have a gun on me. So, I tried to hurry up to get to my car before he came to his senses and shot me. But I got to the car, and he left something, so I went back to give it to him.

"His friend made him come back to his senses and his friend snatched me by the neck and put a gun to my face. Somehow, I started yelling, *'hey this guy's got a gun to my face'*, so people would come out and he wouldn't do anything. The next thing I knew I got away and, in my dream, it was me who was chasing them, and then strangely they were chasing me, and I was jumping over fences to get away.

"Then I was thinking like trying to call you, Dad, to tell you like something may happen to you because these people are coming for me and I have no gun and they are following me, trying to get me.

"Then the next thing I know I was with Camillo, and I saw like four guys get into a car and I told Camillo do you have a gun. I tried to hide from the guys so they wouldn't see me, and he had a .380 Colt, and l grabbed the gun and crept up to the car and I walked to the window and shot the gun into his face. Then I looked inside the window at the guy who supposedly shot Cody and I shot him too, twice in the face. The gun wasn't killing him. I heard a bang go off, but the shot still wasn't killing them. It was hitting them, but nothing was happening. I realized the gun was junk. It was like a double action .380, a weak caliber.

"Suddenly the dream ended. I was scared a little bit because I felt I had to put my life on the line because of what happened to Cody, and it was scary. Those guys were coming after me because I knew he did it and I got a crazy-like feeling that you did something, and you might not come back. It was crazy like going to war and not coming back. Who would ever think that by living life that you might get killed and it was scary."

Twitch had another dream of Cody but did not reveal it to his father.

Him and Kelley and George were with Cody and Cody was hanging out at the house and he was supposed to die at a certain time that day, and Willie did not want him leaving his house. He was thinking up ways of how to prevent Cody's death. He believed if Cody did not leave the house he would not die. But he didn't tell Cody. But strangely it seemed like Cody may have known. Then the dream suddenly ended. And again, leaving Twitch imbibed with bone-chilling thoughts.

Twitch realized some dreams made no sense while others accurately predicted the future.

Almost two months after Cody died, Twitch knew he had to immerse himself in his job to take his mind off Cody. He was still taking Cody's death extraordinarily hard, and it seemed to be getting worse. He had to change jobs and started working for USA Air-Conditioning and loved his first day at work. But by the third day, about eleven o'clock, he called his father who was at the gym.

"Hi, son," his father said. "How's your job today?"

"It's fine," Twitch said. "But I'm sad."

"Oh, son, really," his father said full of compassion. He knew what his son was sad about and knew he could not do anything about it so kept it to himself. "Tell me what you're sad about? That's what I'm here for."

"I can't take my mind off Cody. I've been thinking about him all morning. I'm so sad."

"I know, son," his father said. "I'm sad too. I just didn't speak about it. I've been thinking about him all morning."

Tears came to his father's eyes. He could tell his son was suffering. He had to save his son's sanity.

"I feel all alone with Cody gone. I have no one to speak to. And I have no one to call when I do something good. Before I would call Cody and say, *'Hey, I did this or that and I'm really happy.'* And Cody would say how happy he was for me.

"Then Cody would do the same to me. He would have me to call when he did something good. He was so happy to stop selling drugs and have his job at Home Depot and called me and said, *'Hey Twitch come see me work and I'm really happy.'* And I would say how happy I was for him." Twitch's grief was tormenting him endlessly. "Cody's gone. I have no one to talk to anymore. I feel alone," he said again.

"I understand, son. Cody was a big loss. I took his death hard too."

"I know you did, Dad."

"It really hurt me."

"He didn't have to die like that. He gave his life for his friends, but his friends wouldn't give their life for him. He was probably so dedicated and loyal to his friends because he was an only child, just like me, and hoped if he took care of them, they would take care of him. He had no one and wanted someone just like me. He just wanted to be close to his friends so he could have someone. Me and Cody had a lot in common. He was an only child, just like me."

He wanted to help his son but what could he do? How could he ease his grief? And by seeing his son grieve it intensified his own grieving. He was taking Cody's death just as hard. His father wondered if Twitch would recover.

"He didn't have to die," his father said. "Yet he did die." His father was praying his son would recover.

"He was betrayed by them. Kelley and George betrayed him."

"Cody's betrayal was the biggest betrayal I ever seen in my life. Yet he spoke good about them like he did to everybody. If he just knew what happened after he died, he would be devastated to know his friends were not his friends."

"Cody was intelligent," Twitch said. "Not like George and Kelley."

"I know he was intelligent. That's why he spoke good about everybody. Kelley and George are stupid. They were beneath Cody. Cody should have never hung with people like that."

"I'll never deal with them again, even though I do still have some love for Kelley." Then he got quiet for a few seconds. "I feel like killing George. But I know I can't shoot him. And the niggas that killed Cody, I would like to shoot them too."

"I would like to shoot those niggas too." He had to pacify his son and at the same time, be sure his son would not do it. "It's not your duty to shoot them. You weren't there. Let *Crime Stoppers* handle the case. They'll pick up the punks."

"George and Kelley should be the ones to go after them. They should have gone after them the same night. Kelley told me repeatedly he was going after them, but it's been months now and he's done nothing and still talking that nonsense. He's not going after anybody. He's all talk."

"I know. I can sense it."

Twitch repeated to his father several more times how sad he was, and his father was sad for him and wished he could help him and get justice for Cody as well.

"I don't have any more friends," Twitch said again. "My life's been changed forever."

"What do you mean?"

"Cody's gone. He's never coming back. The way my life was with Cody is different now. It will never be the same. And it will never come back. I'll never see him again."

"You're right, son. I understand what you mean now. But please take it easy."

"I don't have anybody but you. When you die, I'll be all alone."

"I have this feeling I'm going to be around for a long time."

"I hope so."

"And after I'm gone you will probably have a family of your own by then."

"I don't know, Dad."

Twitch went immediately back to talking about Cody.

"It destroyed my life. I feel I lost something. I feel lonely. I can't call Cody when I get a house to tell him to come over."

Twitch was really suffering now. His hatred was overwhelming his sadness.

"It makes me want to go back there. It makes me want to whack somebody.

"When I think of Cody, what did he feel when he got shot? When he looked down. Seen the holes in his chest. Shot four times. Walked up to Kelley like saying, *I'm shot! I'm shot!* It's real.

"I was thinking like, where he will go? Where did he go after he died? And now I think where I will go when I die. It changed my whole life. It made me bad. I feel compelled to be bad and justified to kill the niggas who killed Cody. It left a scar on me, that will never go away. It makes me teary. Every time I think of Cody it makes me sadder, like I have to take a gasp of air.

"And my life is unbelievable now. Nothing will be the same. As I said, I have no one but you."

His father listened sadly, refusing to interrupt his ranting. Certainly, his son was so traumatized he was scarred for life.

"What I don't understand why Kelley didn't help Cody. Okay, he didn't have a gun to shoot it out with the killer, which is understandable, but I'm going to say the same thing you said repeatedly. He could have calmed Cody down, told him to lie down as well as help him lie down, instead of letting him collapse to the floor. Kelley could have tried to stop the bleeding, position Cody where his wounds were pointing upwards, stemming the flow of blood. And most importantly, staying by his side till the police arrived, and giving the police as much information as possible to apprehend the killer. But instead, he told me verbally, him and George got in the crowd and watched Cody, mortally wounded, fighting for his life, from the sidelines.

"It doesn't make sense to me to watch your friend dying and not helping him. Nobody was expecting him to fight an armed killer while he was unarmed. But at least, stay by his side and tend to his needs. Afterall, this was a life and death situation.

"Son, you may not understand but I'm enraged myself."

"I do understand."

"Even when they wheeled Cody out to the helicopter, Kelley still offered no help to the police. I guess I'll never understand. You don't watch your friend die unless you are involved in it. Detective Madero thinks Kelley may have been the shooter, even though I doubt it."

"You're making my situation worse, Dad."

"Okay, son, I'll stop talking about it."

"Maybe you need a girlfriend. At least you will have her."

Twitch did not want to talk about a girlfriend. He missed Cody. Cody was the only thing on his mind right now.

"Dad, what made things worse I was listening to the rap *Dawgs for Life* by the rapper *DMX*, and one of his lyrics went like this, '*Remember life is our hood but the caskets are all wood and we all take it there someday. We're here on Sunday and could be gone on Monday....*'

"Dad, I was shocked, because I was listening to it on Sunday when Cody went out and found out he was gone on Monday. Killed just like that."

"Really? I'm shocked too."

"It just seemed so unreal."

His father wanted to help his emotionally devastated son. He was in intense mourning. The only thought was to get him to a psychological counselor.

"Maybe you should see a psychiat rist."

"What for? What could he do for me?"

"Ease your grief, give you medication of some type."

"Okay, but not like the last one."

His father was happy his son was willing to see a psychiatrist.

"I'll take care of it later today," his father said.

"Another thing, I was thinking that maybe Cody died thinking I didn't care about him; didn't care if he got murdered. Maybe he thinks I wouldn't feel bad for him."

"I don't think so, son. That's a sign of self-inflicted guilt. You have nothing to feel guilty about. You've done nothing wrong. If there is some form of life after death, Cody knows you feel bad for him. And he knows you cared about him, and you were a good friend and suffered that you lost him."

"Cody went his way. I went my way. But we were still friends and were in contact often. We didn't need to call each other every day to know we were friends.

"My friend is gone, erased from the earth. I lost something I'll never get back. That's what I feel like with Cody gone.

"I'm more alone in this world than ever. George and Kelley. They let me down. George got my friend killed. I have no one now. Life don't mean nothing by yourself.

"I keep a gun because I'm mad. I feel my life got altered. I carry a gun for revenge. When they killed my friend, it makes me want to kill somebody black. When I heard my friend died, it made me lose value for my life."

The grief was too much for Twitch. His father had to comfort his son.

"We cannot take the law into our own hands. If we could, the first one I would shoot is George. Crime Stoppers will solve it. I'm certain they will no matter how long it takes."

He had no faith in Crime Stoppers. Nobody had faith in Crime Stoppers. All he could do is wait and see.

His life was full of tragedy, death, and violence. He had chosen that way of life. His father never raised him like that.

Willie had to end it. He could not take it anymore. The grief was going to kill him.

"Dad, I got to get back to work. I'll call you later."

"Okay, try to take it easy until then."

"I'll do my best."

They hung up. His father got back to working out, with the sadness of Cody burdening his mind as it had been for months now. There was just something that enraged him when Cody got shot in the back. It was like attacking a man when he was sleeping, and any man could fall victim. His younger brother had died in the same manner as Cody and to this day it still enraged him.

The world was full of cowards, and droves of cowards were arriving every second of the day and night, thinking nothing of shooting an unarmed man in the back.

Cowards were born cowards. You could not change them. They could not change themselves. It was in their DNA. You had to let cowards be cowards and leave it at that. They were a hopeless breed of scum. The only solution was to kill them all.

Twitch sat on the floor with his back against the wall, still relentlessly mourning Cody's death. Cody's death had left him haunted, heartbroken, horror-stricken, full of hatred. Vengeance never ceased corrupting his mind. How he would love to kill Cody's killer, but who was he, and where could he find him? He had the courage but not the ignorance to commit murder. It would solve nothing.

And the terrifying dreams never ceased. That afternoon Twitch finally fell into a pleasant slumber. Without realizing it, he instantly started dreaming. He was soaring over the land and ocean, and he was fishing and was happy for a change. He wished his happiness would last a lifetime. But to his dismay, it changed in a flash. He got a phone call and to his horror it was Cody.

Twitch had to verify this torment once and for all and said, "I know you're dead, Cody!"

And Cody responded, "No I'm not, cuz. Hang up and call me back. I'll prove I'm not dead."

And when Twitch hung up and called him back Cody answered the phone.

"You are dead, Cody!"

"If I was dead, why would I be answering the phone?"

Then Twitch woke up, shivering in horror from head to toe. But he stayed in bed and unconsciously dozed off again. And the phone rang again. He snatched it up in a frenzy and answered. It was Cody.

"You're dead, Cody! Why are you doing this to me?"

"I just want to talk to you, cuz."

Twitch was a little relieved. Cody did not deny his death. And he knew Cody was dead.

"I had nothing to do with your death, Cody!"

"I just want to talk to you, cuz," Cody said again as if he was alive. "You're the only friend I have. George is a coward and Kelley left me to die."

And again, Twitch began to wonder if Cody was really alive. His mind had to be playing games on him.

Twitch woke back up with a terrible jolt, and this time smartly got out of bed. He began to wonder if there was a dimension where the dead were not dead. And if there was, what would it be like?

Would it be a dream world? Would it be a tangible world? Would it be a spirit world?

His dreams and thoughts and conflicting feelings of Cody's death were killing him. Could he ever extricate the hurt lingering in his heart.

Probably not, because it was almost two years now, and instead of his grief diminishing, it was actually growing.

Later that day, Twitch was growing tired. He was afraid to go to bed, for he may have more dreams of Cody. How many would it take before it killed him?

Twitch slowly closed his eyes, keeping them partly open, praying he would not fall back into a dream world.

Without realizing it, as usual, he fell back into a deep sleep, and it immediately thrust him back into dreaming. But thinking he was awake and in control of himself, he felt comfortable and relaxed and basked in joy. He wished it would last for an eternity. But to his disappointment, it was short-lived, because Cody called again.

Twitch spoke before Cody had a chance, "We're still looking for your killer, Cody!"

"You mean you haven't found him yet?" Cody sounded disappointed.

And to Twitch's relief, the dream and the sound of Cody's voice faded away. Twitch awoke, but this time, not in fear.

He lay in bed, looking up at the ceiling, while pondering Cody's death. After Cody's death depression seized him worse than ever. He could not bear the grief of tragedies any longer. He would have to grieve alone, because he had no one other than his father to confide in.

He immediately summoned his father and told him of the new dreams of Cody, and how Cody sounded surprised that they had not found his killer.

"It seems as if there is life after death," his father said in deep thought.

"It would be nice if there was," Twitch responded.

Over the last two years, Twitch had often attempted to contact Cody's mother without success. He tried contacting Cody's Aunt Shayne, and she brushed him off repeatedly. He knew his contact with them was over forever. So, Twitch never called Cody's mother again. Nor did he ever call Aunt Shayne again. The handwriting was on the wall. They wanted nothing to do with him. Cody was dead because of his friends.

And his father explained it all to him and the reasons why they avoided him.

"Son, they are perceiving you in the same manner as they perceive George and Kelley, although you were not there. They have to blame Cody's death on someone, and they have a damn good reason to. George set up Cody's death and Kelley made no attempt to help Cody as he lay there dying." He looked profoundly at his son. He did not want to hurt him further. "If Cody's friends let him die, what makes you think they would see you differently. They probably think you would have reacted no differently and let Cody die too. We both know you are not like those guys, because I never raised you to be. You would have never set up Cody to be killed and you would have helped Cody. And that concludes everything, so don't feel bad if they never deal with you again."

"Okay, Dad," Twitch said. "I understand." And the subject of Cody was dropped for the time being.

Months later, on Cody's twenty-fourth birthday, Twitch was compelled to attempt to contact Cody's mother. He could not get himself to call her, so he resolved to text her. Twitch, surprised, immediately received a response and was euphoric.

No sooner had he finished reading her text, when Cody's mother called him. Twitch was smiling in delight as they talked for a while.

She praised Twitch for being a true friend. He thanked her repeatedly. She assured him she would never forget his concern for Cody. He was ecstatic beyond explanation.

A few seconds later, unsurprisingly to Twitch, she fell back into mourning. Twitch just listened to her weeping, feeling horrible, wishing he could do something to allay her grief. Time was the only cure.

Twitch's love and compassion for Cody's mother was so intense he would have stayed on the phone with her forever, but she ended the conversation for her own good.

They hung up after promising they would stay in touch.

Twitch had refrained from calling Crime Stoppers for a long time, especially since Detective Maderos never made any substantial gains on solving Cody's murder. It was one nonsensical excuse after another. *He could not just say I'm baffled, and can't solve the murder,* Twitch thought. *He had too much pride.* But the detective himself had to admit he was probably not trying hard enough. With all the tips and information coming in by numerous witnesses, he still could not solve the murder. *What a disgrace,* Twitch thought.

Or was Detective Maderos guilty of dereliction of duty and that was the actual reason for his failure to crack the case and arrest the killer?

Finally, months later, anger was starting to overwhelm Twitch's grief since Detective Mederos still had made no progress in solving Cody's death. To complicate matters further, the bulletin of Cody's murder was taken offline for no apparent reason. Twitch knew if he did not take action, it could turn into a cold case and never be solved.

Twitch grabbed the phone and dialed Crime Stoppers. After being transferred from department to department, he finally got to speak with a case worker. To Twitch's disappointment it took about a half-hour before they even came up with Cody's information.

Finally, a Detective Santos got on the phone and informed Twitch Detective Mederos retired and the case was passed over to him. He told Twitch to stay on the line until he called and consulted with Detective Mederos. It was another half-hour before Detective Santos returned. Detective Santos informed Twitch he did not know much about the case and said he would call back as soon as he got more information.

Twitch was feeling almost hopeless now, losing confidence by the second. He was convinced they did not care if they solved Cody's murder. And if he did not badger them, they never would. *How pitiful,* Twitch thought.

The next day he called Twitch.

"Okay, I have more information now," Detective Santos said. "Detective Mederos and myself concluded that Cody's death came from friendly fire."

Twitch was shocked. He knew they were referring to Kelley again. The day after the killing, Detective Mederos called and asked if Kelley had a beef with Cody. He believed that Kelley shot Cody.

In Twitch's mind, it could not be Kelley, but evidence was pointing that way.

"Really," Twitch said. "But it couldn't be."

"The trajectory of the bullets traced it to friendly fire." Detective Santos was adamant. Then he became a little threatening. "And anybody holding back information on the case can face charges."

Twitch knew Detective Santos was insinuating if he knew anything about the case, he better give it now or face jail later. He wished he knew something that could solve Cody's murder. Maybe the detective was implying he knew Kelley was the murderer. Whatever he was suggesting about Kelley was preposterous. Twitch knew the best tactic was to ignore it and try to throw him on track of the real perpetrator.

"I don't know why you aren't trying to solve the murder," Twitch said.

"We are trying. There just isn't any evidence at the moment." Detective Santos was growing agitated with Twitch with every word coming out of his mouth.

"On the night of the murder, I got a tip from a girl that was there and said the killer was Jerry and gave it to Detective Maderos."

""Yes, you did, and Detective Maderos told you he spoke with her, and she admitted she did not actually see him do it. So that tip is out of the question. We can't arrest a murder suspect on hearsay."

Twitch could tell by Detective Santos' tone of voice he was annoying him.

"What if we put up a reward?"

That was more than enough for Detective Santos. He was about to explode. His patience with Twitch was rapidly waning. Then he questioned Twitch in an unusually rude manner.

"Who are you?"

"Cody's best friend."

"If a reward is offered, we will be flooded with calls from every person trying to get it and all that shit."

When Twitch heard the detective use the word *'shit'* he knew the detective was getting angry.

"Almost all the calls will be nonsense or lies and won't even be related to the case. The callers will just be trying to get free money. So, a reward is out of the question."

Twitch recognized Detective Santos' anger instantly. He was not sure if it was a tactic by the detective to make up a reason why they could not solve Cody's murder or because they did not want to solve it.

Twitch felt he understood the detective explicitly. He did not want to solve it. Twitch wondered if they were friends with the owner of The Boss Mansion where Cody died or were they being paid off for some inconspicuous reason?

"I understand," Twitch said, not wanting to anger the detective further.

Maybe this detective will try to link him to the murder even though he was not there. Maybe Detective Santo would possibly take a false admission of guilt from anybody just to get rid of Cody's case.

"We'll do everything we can to solve this case," Detective Santos told Twitch.

"Okay," Twitch said. "I'll call back periodically."

"Okay." They hung up.

Twitch, as soon as he saw his father, told him of his conversation with Detective Santos. His father agreed with Twitch that maybe they could not or did not want to solve the case.

Twitch also told his father that when Cody's Aunt Shayne learned that the owner of The Boss Mansion was a Yahweh, she thought that maybe the Yahwehs murdered Cody and had enough influence with the police to make them overlook the murder.

When Cody was airlifted to the hospital it was only an attempted murder. After Cody died it became a murder charge and when the police came back to The Boss Mansion for a forensics investigation, the owner would not let them in. So, the police had to wait for hours to get a court order before they could enter. That in itself should tell her the Yahwehs had no connection with the police.

But Aunt Shayne never strayed from her belief the Yahwehs may have been involved. The more research she did on the Yahwehs the more convinced she was.

Twitch's father told him to explain to Aunt Shayne that years ago he had befriended members of the Yahwehs and knew them fairly well and doubted that they were involved. Although the Yahwehs, hosted the party and owned The Boss Mansion, they had nothing to gain by killing an innocent young white man. It made no sense for the Yahwehs to kill Cody. He had done nothing wrong to them. The Yahwehs, were also friends with most white people.

They probably denied the police access to their home because they had a bad relationship with them.

During the 1990s, the Yahwehs began helping the poor and revamping the ghettos, and they had gained nationally and internationally recognition. Today they were just a typical religious sect struggling to survive.

So, Twitch's father hoped he eased the mind of Cody's family by reassuring them that, although he had no reliable proof, the Yahwehs most likely had no part in their son's murder.

Twitch was still suffering miserably over Cody's death. His father decided to rationalize with him, hoping to ease his mind by explaining an issue in Cody's life that effected Twitch as well.

"Son, you can't spend the rest of your life mourning over something you have no control over."

"I know. But Cody's death is just torturing me. I'm not sure if I'll ever get over it."

"You have to," his father said. "You can't go on living like that."

"But what can I do?" Twitch asked.

His father tilted his head pensively, taking a deep breath.

"Son, as you know Cody was an only child, just like you. I'm sure you understand that there are negative characteristics of being an only child."

Twitch was listening intently, having an idea of what his father was going to say.

"Of course."

"For an only child, psychologists have researched and concluded that the absence of siblings can be detrimental to a child's emotional and psychological wellbeing. Onlies are often labeled as being drastically lonely, struggle to form friendships, self-centered, less empathetic, and more anxious than those with siblings."

"Okay," Twitch said. "So, what are you driving at?"

"An only child often tries to turn friends into siblings, which is the biggest mistake in the world. And this is where Cody went wrong without knowing it."

"You know, it's funny you say that because I've seen myself doing just that."

"It's a dead-end road. Friends today is equivalent to enemies and that is what Cody had in his life, a bunch of enemies who only care about themselves.

"Cody was unaware of this and always saw himself as a protector of his friends and lost his life while trying to defend his friends. Cody showed the utmost dedication and respect to his friends. Yet his friends not only showed no respect to Cody but let him die for them when they would never die for him.

"He lived for them and by looking at life the way he wanted and not the way it truly was, he died for them, senselessly. And, at twenty-two- years-old, his life was taken when he was shot multiple times."

"But, Dad," Twitch said. "You're giving me a story I already know."

"Exactly," his father said. "And I'm doing that so hopefully you will never make the same mistake. Making friends into family and believing they are family, and believing they feel toward you, the way you feel toward them, is nothing more, nothing less, than a delusion. You will die for your friends while believing they are family is a gradual descent into Hell. Because they will never die for you, and they don't look at you as family. There is no such thing as friends today and Cody's death is a prime example for you to learn from."

"You're right, Dad," Twitch said. "They'll let me die the way they let Cody die." Twitch had tears in his eyes. "They could have at least run to the police and gave them as much information as they could to pick up the niggas that shot Cody."

"They could have done a lot of things and did nothing," his father interrupted. "Good for nothing guys!"

"Cody must have cried when he realized that nobody had his back, and he was dying. Then nobody coming forward to help apprehend the killer could make anybody cry."

"I know I would have cried," his father said. "My friends, my so-called family, turned their backs on me and let me die. I would have cried my eyes out had I had the time."

Twitch was overwhelmed with emotion as he repeated sadly. "Nobody coming forward to help apprehend the killer."

Just hearing his father say he would have cried almost made him cry, not because he was sad for his father, but because he knew his father's words were fact. They let Cody die.

"It was a disgrace upon disgrace," his father said. "George and Kelley have to live with that." Then his father took the initiative to further explain Cody's situation. "You're doing something Cody did and it's a big mistake."

"Really," Twitch said. "What's that?"

"Cody's friends as well as your friends are right out ghetto. And that's a disaster in itself. Let me explain. The risk for violent crimes later in life is elevated among *only* children. If perinatal or parental risks were combined with being an only child, the odds ratios for violent offending increased four-fold to eight-fold. And now you are among ghetto people, and without realizing it, your chances of engaging in violent crimes is intensified by ten-fold, especially when you look at them as family. I didn't make all this up, but I can sense a lot of it."

Twitch was somber, ruminating, in deep thought, assimilating what his father was saying. "Are you saying Cody is dead because of his choice of friends?"

"To a certain degree, yes," his father said. "But more so because he turned his choice of friends into family."

Twitch was thinking further in his and Cody's past. They were both only children. And they both followed similar lives.

"Are you also implying that parents who make an *only* child are not making good decisions by not following up with siblings for that child? And are you implying that the parents who make an only child are not thinking rationally and are possibly liable for their only child going astray and leading a life of crime, even getting murdered, though the child may be intelligent? And had Cody had siblings he may be alive today."

His father was pleased Twitch explained it better to him than he could have explained it to Twitch. "Not exactly, but at the same time you can say the parents are instrumental in the child's outcome. From what I surmised, is that when parents make an only child it's usually due to either economics or selfishness. If they can't afford more than one child, they settle for one child and their reasoning is correct at that moment, but they are oblivious of the devastating emotional effect it will have upon the child later. If it's selfishness, they don't want the headache of raising more than a single child.

"See, as I just mentioned, Cody's and your friends are ghetto and ghetto people have no sense of loyalty and they are always trying to use somebody, and the reason is rudimentary, because the typical intellect level in a ghetto is substantially below average. Race has little to *do* with this though — intelligent people flee poor places and cluster where possible high incomes, quality shelter, and low crime rates are common. Sadly, the dire circumstances in a ghetto self-perpetuate as the people there have children. They make babies for sport and prestige and welfare benefits. Some parents train their children to be beggars, while the more deranged parents exploit their offspring for drugs and prostitution.

"A ghetto is a low intellect gene pool. Spending money attempting to educate people in ghettos is a waste. Working with people whose IQ is 75 and who would be lucky to get a F+ on any academic test. A better use for this money would be to provide some sort of social welfare benefit in which all citizens of a ghetto population regularly receive an income in the form of a payment, without working a job. That's the only hope for the poor people with ghetto mentalities."

Twitch was pensive, suffused in thought. "I never thought about that. I never knew that way of life was possible. You mean to just give them money and let them stay uneducated and stupid?"

"Exactly," his father said. "And stay away from those kinds of fools or you may end up dead like Cody."

"But Cody was intelligent."

"Of course, he was intelligent, but made the fatal mistake of making his ghetto friends into family. It could happen to anybody, mainly to only children though." Now was his chance to really dissuade Twitch from doing that. "When an intelligent person befriends ghetto mentality people, that person is usually suffering from a self-esteem problem, where he sees himself at the level of his ghetto friends. And if you don't stop doing that it will turn into a disaster for you. Just remember, you can't put trust and friendship into a ghetto relationship."

Twitch went silent, more introspective than ever, as he assimilated his father's indoctrination of what friends were. If he did not heed his father's advice, he could very well get targeted for death.

"Dad, I hate to say that you are a hundred percent correct. The longer I associate with them the more my life could be in danger."

"It looks like you are starting to see the facts of reality," his father said with a big smile. His words seemed to be swaying Twitch's thoughts toward the right path. If he heeded them, he should be alive for a long time.

Then Twitch's mind flashed to Cody and the Blacks again.

Cody was the only child on the mother's side of the Clayville family. The Clayville family had no one to carry on the family name. It was disaster upon disaster.

As Twitch ruminated on the Blacks, he concluded that something had to be done to prevent them from murdering Whites. If the police did not protect them, they would have to protect themselves. That meant arming themselves then going into open warfare with them.

Most Whites would never openly mention it, but they knew it had to be done, and it was slowly heading that way.

As twitch got older, due to the tragedies wracking his mind, body, and soul, he began to look scragglier and more ill-kempt than ever. His hair was long and straggly, beard and mustache growing so thick that they joined together and appeared like a single attachment, and his dirty, ragged clothes looked like he found them in a garbage dumpster. But that paled next to his wild imagination.

He believed he could fight the Blacks all alone and that the Blacks were afraid of him. Actually, he could tell they were afraid of him. He would deliberately make eye contact with them, and they would quickly glance downward until he passed. Twitch needed no further evidence. The proof was in their actions. And to boost his confidence, he had a duffle bag full of loaded pistols, from a 9 mm. to a .22. And he would use them without hesitation if the Blacks provoked him.

But it was nonsensical. No black man was afraid of him. Because no black man even knew who he was. Most of the danger in society was with the Blacks who were so devious and treacherous they would shoot anybody in the back and stupidly claim a victory, after fabricating an incredible story of fighting off an entire army alone.

Without even knowing it, he was becoming blinded to reality.

Despite the ignorance of the ghetto Blacks, once they were aware they could get away with murder, they were so emboldened, they not only killed each other in broad daylight, but now started killing more white people without a care. They knew the police would not arrest them, because the government told them not to, and the government ruled the police. The most logical reason the government overlooked most of the killings, was because they wanted the slaughter to continue. As long as Blacks killed Blacks and sometimes killed unimportant Whites, it was okay. The less ghetto Blacks alive made life safer for the so-called decent white people.

Sadly, with the passing of time, Twitch and Kelley were becoming more distant with each other. Twitch did make an effort to stay friends, but he could sense Kelley was hoping he would simply disappear from his life. Kelley felt that Twitch was out to get him for revenge over Cody's death. Twitch and Cody were lifelong friends and Kelley was worried Twitch might kill him. Twitch never failed to carry his gun and always had it at the ready.

More terrifying to Kelley was that every time Twitch saw him, he would make Kelley give him another rundown on Cody's death. Kelley had all rights to believe Twitch and his father felt he was either a conspirator in Cody's death or knew who killed Cody or personally killed Cody. Afterall, he did refuse to speak with homicide for two years now. That was a reason for Twitch or anybody else to believe he was involved.

Once Twitch asked Kelley to meet him to discuss Cody again and he agreed but told Twitch to meet him at the entrance of Broward Health Hospital.

Twitch and his father both interpreted this as fear that Kelley was certain Twitch was gunning for him and wanted to be at the hospital to get medical treatment if this nightmare came true. Twitch discussed this with his father, and both were saddened Kelley felt this way but felt Kelley's fear was a confession in disguise that he was involved in Cody's murder.

Twitch felt bad and called Kelley multiple time, but Kelley ignored his calls for weeks. Then surprisingly one day, Kelley did answer the phone, and he told Kelley he would never bring harm to him. Over the next couple days Twitch contacted Kelley and again assured Kelley, he would never harm him. Kelley appeared a little relieved but still wished Twitch would just disappear and he would never see him again.

Realistically, Kelley did not fully believe Twitch. He wanted nothing to do with Twitch but never admitted it. His behavior showed it.

As more time passed, Twitch's father seen Kelley in Publix one night and had a brief talk with him and mentioned he was happy to see Kelley again. He could tell Kelley was nervous by his jerky body movements and fast speech and wanted to get as far away from him as possible. It was raining and lightning, so Twitch's father offered Kelley a ride to his hotel room. He would not be able to sleep at night if he made Kelly trudge through the rain and chance the lightning.

Kelley thanked him as he was dropped off at Motel 6.

When he got home, he told Twitch he seen Kelley and could tell Kelley had changed a lot for the worse. He did not seem himself anymore and interpreted this to Twitch that Kelley was suffering from a combination of fear and guilt, and it was more obvious than ever Kelley would never be the same.

It seemed to hurt Twitch, but he agreed with his father. Kelley was a changed man for life.

Weeks later, Twitch again stopped hearing from Kelley, and he was prompted to look online to see if Kelley had gotten arrested again. And sure enough, there was Kelly's mugshot.

Months later Kelley was released and told Twitch that right before he got out, a Miami homicide detective paid him a visit and questioned him extensively on Cody's murder.

Kelley was as truthful as he could be, and the homicide detective ruled him as not a suspect in Cody's death.

Twitch and his father were both happy. But that did not make his father look at Kelley any differently. He still wanted nothing to do with him.

For the hundredth time, Twitch's father told him, "If it was you that got killed that night, George and Kelley would be pumping me full of the same shit they pumped Cody's mother full of."

"I know," Twitch answered. He was sincere, because he knew it was the truth.

"It's not that they lied to her, it's just they refused to tell her all the facts."

"I know," Twitch said again. "I know they told her what they wanted her to know. If Cody would have lived, he would have killed both of them."

"And George," his father said. "I wouldn't have even talked with him had it been you who died. He's the biggest damn liar in the world. Do you see him on Instagram anymore?"

"All the time," Twitch said. "He's been back on Instagram with that big shitty smile on his face, as if nothing happened. Matter of fact, I heard he's using Cody's death as a status symbol to boost his cowardly reputation around the neighborhood by claiming he was involved in a shootout, and someone was killed."

Twitch and his father fell silent in disgust and grief. Was George even a human? If he was human, he was a human without a soul.

The only thing Cody's mother and Twitch could do was give up on George, for he was a hopeless case.

Twitch was still overwhelmed with grief and rage since Cody's killer had not yet been apprehended, and Detective Santos of homicide continued to make every excuse imaginable and unimaginable for not solving Cody's murder.

He could not just say he was bordering on incompetency like Detective Maderos, and could not solve it, and should find a new career. Twitch began to wonder if Detective Santos had even solved a single murder.

Detective Santos had a sly streak in him, just like Detective Maderos, and constantly told Cody's mother and Twitch, the same old story they told from the very beginning, that it was becoming obvious it was a banal and worn-out defensive tactic: Cody's death came from friendly fire, but they stopped short of saying the killer was Kelley since Kelley was interrogated in jail and was ruled not a suspect.

Cody's mother and twitch were so sick of hearing the silliness of the determination, they began to ignore it. Since Kelley was no longer a suspect who would they accuse next? It could not be George because George vanished like most cowards when the shooting started. So, it was obvious the detective's alleged findings was false and a way to keep covering himself and now the story was preposterous and miserably bogus; it had too many holes in it.

As the years were slipping away, Twitch finally accepted he had to learn to live with the grief that may never go away or face a lifetime of misery and destroy his own life. He thought of Cody. Cody would not want that.

The tormenting thought of the ghetto nigga who had murdered Cody, intensified his rage. Twitch reasoned that even if the nigga was never brought to justice, he would pay some way, someday, directly or indirectly. He may pay even without realizing he was paying for the senseless murder of a young man who was as innocent as any man can be.

Twitch was losing all faith, not only in Detective Santos, but in Miami's entire homicide division. The biggest disgrace homicide committed came a couple months after Cody's murder when his Death Notice was taken offline and after an additional two years, was never put back on the internet, as if he never existed. It was an indication Cody's murder was becoming a cold case.

Twitch was pensive, reflective, heartbroken, as every passing moment reignited his grief and anger. As he relived the senselessness of Cody's murder, for the thousandth time, and the obvious incompetence of the homicide units to solve it was devastating.

The killer was not even evading homicide, for his murderous ways proved he was not smart enough. Homicide had obviously placed the wrong detectives on the case or was deliberately blocking it, was the only assessment Twitch could conjure up.

How could homicide not solve this murder that scores of bystanders and partygoers witnessed? Many people were firsthand eyewitnesses to the murder, yet Detective Santos was as stumped in solving it as if he was walking around in the dark.

Twitch's grief was so intense it was goading him on to see justice prevail, to ensure that Cody's murder was not overlooked or forgotten and that his killer was arrested and sent to prison or executed for his murderous ways. Twitch believed that Cody's murderer had killed again or even multiple times since he murdered Cody, for killers did not kill today for no reason then never kill again. Killers, like most criminals, were recidivists and egomaniacs who were compelled to continue on their legacy of murder until captured or killed themselves. The only solution was to eradicate them from society.

What infuriated Twitch still more, was that Cody's mother was still in terrible mourning and each time he contacted her, her emotions would dictate her reasoning, and she would become hysterically grief-stricken, and homicide had neither detained a suspect, nor, at least, pinpointed a suspect?

More for Cody's mother than himself, and despite homicide's lack of progress, he prayed Cody's murder would not be relegated to a cold case, stashed away in a file and never solved, ignored and forever forgotten.

The rage burned inside him so intensely that it precipitated a fantasy of vengeance; if he got his hands on that despicable son of a bitch, cowardly killer, he would take the law into his own hands and mete out the proper type of justice.

A rope around the coward's neck, slowly torturing him, slowly lynching him, slowly lifting him off the ground just enough for his feet to scrape the grass, as he gagged and strangled and ultimately seeing his life fading away.

A quick death would be too good for that despicable bastard. And disposing of him would not only be an act of justice; it would be a boon to society, one less killer walking the streets.

Someday justice would prevail. It was inevitable. And Twitch could not wait.

Although Twitch's emotions were running wild, he suddenly developed a soft spot in his heart for Detective Santos, driving him toward more rationality as a profound analysis was settling in him. He had to be fair to Detective Santos and should stop condemning him, because it may not be him.

In retrospect, he kept coming to the same conclusion. Could it be homicide did not want to solve the murder. Could it be homicide did not want Detective Santos to solve the murder? Could it be homicide thwarting Detective Santos' investigation so he could not solve the murder? In this day and age anything was believable, and the passing of time would tell.

All he could do now was wait and see.

Almost three long years had elapsed, with no sign of Cody's murder being solved, not only kept eating away at his mother's sanity, but had transmuted itself into an everlasting rage, and as it had done to Twitch, invoked in her a desire for vengeance she never knew she had.

She envisioned herself finding and kidnapping the murderer and slowly and deliberately chopping him up in pieces. Hearing his screams and rants for mercy would be music to her ears. The torment and thirst for revenge was so unbearable she would continue mutilating the nigga killer, rolling him over on his stomach and taking a butcher knife and stabbing him four times in the back where each stab, the tip of the blade exited his chest, reciprocating the four bullets he pumped into her son's back and exited his chest. She would be gloating as the killer would be screaming in horror as she continued dismembering his body.

She would give the murderer the same mercy, which was none, and treachery, which was a lot, that he gave to her son.

Then she thought of the nigga killer's mother. She wanted to punish his mother too, exact as much vengeance on her as was possible. She wanted his mother to suffer like she suffered. She wanted his mother to know what it felt like losing a son for no sensible reason at all.

And if the nigga's mother was human, she would feel the pain, the way she felt the pain, of losing a child in such a violent and senseless way.

Of course, her pain would forever transcend the mother's pain since Cody was her only child and most nigga mother's, had many children. Then the nigga's mother could carry, at least, some of the same pain and anguish that she carried for her murdered son for the rest of her days, filled with torment and grief.

That would be justice now.

Despite Cody's mother's hunger for vengeance, she suddenly felt reasoning overwhelming her senses. Even if she got her revenge, Cody was never coming back. Even if the killer suffered the same fate as Cody, Cody was never coming back. What would be the sense other than a few moments of pleasure.

Her mind shifted to Detective Santos of the City of Miami Homicide. In her perspective, he was good for nothing, and she no longer revered him. He had a thousand suspects with no concrete evidence on any of them. What was the sense? He avoided her calls, only spoke with her when he accidentally picked up the phone and realized it was Cody's mother. Detective Santos would rush her off the phone with a tirade of insensible excuses. Yeah, obviously, he was good for nothing and did not care about her.

What got her goat the most was that she finally understood, there would be no charges, no arrests. Not while Detective Santos was on the case.

If she lived a hundred years, and shed a million tears, the killer would remain at large, and Detective Santos would still be claiming he was on the verge of solving Cody's murder.

Who was Santos kidding other than himself. She was no fool, even if Santos thought she was, for a fool always believes everybody is a fool.

Then her thoughts shifted to Twitch when he told homicide him and his father wanted to offer a reward for Cody's murderer and Detective Santos went into a semi-rage, telling Twitch to get off that *shit.* He insinuated every scumbag in Miami would be talking *shit,* making up *shit* that would go nowhere, hoping for the reward even though they knew nothing about the murder.

Twitch and his father were baffled by Santos' tirade, unaware if this was fact or fiction.

Miami had its share of scumbags, all right, millions of them, but all of them talking *shit.* It was hard to digest.

Her mind went a step further. What got her goat even more, she believed Miami Homicide never wanted to solve the case. She could sense it, feel it. Homicide was being paid off. Certainly, they were being paid off. And Detective Santos was going along with it.

She no longer had a son. And homicide no longer cared.

What would she do with the rest of her days? She blinked her eyes, felt the thirst for revenge fading, felt the grief stabilizing, and no longer cared.

Nothing mattered anymore. She suddenly felt strange now, as if something was descending upon her. Her eyes burned but no tears fell. Something was happening to her. A lust for life filled her like a gushing hose. She wanted to live on and be happy and make Cody happy.

Optimism vanquished pessimism and she felt stranger. She was optimistic and exalting in the midst of grief? It bemused her.

A realization finally settled upon her, even if she was the mother of a murdered child, even if Detective Santos never solved the murder, nor wanted to solve it, even if the debilitating grief followed her to the grave, it would never again ruin her life, nor shorten her life, for she wanted to live on more than ever, not just for herself but for Cody too.

Justice would somehow, someday, someway prevail. The killer would be apprehended, or nature would mete out justice to him, punishing him with death or tormenting him with guilt and shame, but it was no longer her problem. It was the killer's problem.

Acceptance of her son's death finally settled upon her. She was exalting, would be for the rest of her life.

She could live on in peace, *at last.*

James Haddad is the author of the Wall Street Journal bestselling novel, *Eyes of a Child.* He is a former journalist for the St. Croix Avis Newspaper and is a columnist for Today Magazine. He is a former candidate for the Florida State Senate. He obtained bachelor's and master's degrees from Florida International University.

www.ingramcontent.com/pod-product-compliance
Lightning Source LLC
Chambersburg PA
CBHW030611310726
48979CB00003B/658
* 9 7 8 1 8 9 2 9 8 6 3 5 1 *